I TEXT DEAD PEOPLE

ALSO BY ROSE COOPER

The Blogtastic! Novels

Gossip from the Girls' Room

Rumors from the Boys' Room

Secrets from the Sleeping Bag

c. 1

ROSE COOPER

I
TEXT DEAD
PEOPLE

DELACORTE PRESS

Text and interior illustrations copyright © 2015 by Rose Cooper
Cover art copyright © 2015 by Rose Cooper

randomhousekids.com

Educators and librarians, for a variety of teaching tools, visit us at
RHTeachersLibrarians.com

Library of Congress Cataloging-in-Publication Data
Cooper, Rose
I text dead people / Rose Cooper. — First edition.
pages cm
Summary: "As if living in a creepy house on cemetery grounds weren't horrible enough, Annabel accidentally becomes a guide that bridges the gap between the living and the dead with her cell phone. Which means she is pestered by the deceased 24/7. And until she helps them with their absurd unresolved issues and ridiculous requests, no one will be able to rest in peace"—Provided by publisher.
ISBN 978-0-385-74391-4 (hc) — ISBN 978-0-375-99138-7 (glb) —
ISBN 978-0-385-37321-0 (ebook) [1. Dead—Fiction. 2. Future life—Fiction. 3. Text messages (Cell phone systems)—Fiction. 4. Schools—Fiction.]
I. Title.
PZ7.C78768Iak 2015
[Fic]—dc23
2014020235

The text of this book is set in 13-point Chaparral Pro.
Jacket design by Tamaye Perry
Interior design by Stephanie Moss

Printed in the United States of America
10 9 8 7 6 5 4 3 2 1
First Edition

TO MOM:

Without you, I wouldn't have these stories to tell, the courage to laugh about the experiences, or the strength to pursue my dreams. Also, I would never have taken those typing classes and my texting skills would be far less impressive.

CHAPTER 1

ANNA

There's no such thing as ghosts.

Ghosts don't exist.

Annabel Craven tried to convince herself that there was no reason to be freaked. But then the wrought-iron gate slammed shut behind her with a loud clunk and she knew she wasn't crazy.

She *definitely* had a reason.

Anna glanced back, shuddering slightly at the sight of the house looming behind her. *Her* house now. Maddsen Manor was run-down and creepy. Something seriously right out of a horror film. The dingy gray paint was flaked and peeling, and the windowpanes were smeared with grime and dirt. The backyard was overgrown with bushes, and brambles reached out like claws, ready to snatch anyone who dared walk too close. It looked like it had been abandoned for several years, not just a few months.

Looking at it made Anna's heart sink.

When she and her mom had gotten the news that they'd inherited a mansion from her mom's estranged uncle, Anna had thought it would mean leaving behind their cramped one-bedroom apartment, getting away from the bad memories and the awful luck that always seemed to follow them. She hadn't realized their fresh start would include living in a small town where the dead outnumbered the living.

Turning away, she forced herself to keep walking, her eyes darting nervously around the deserted graveyard. She couldn't shake the feeling that she was being watched. But that was impossible. The mansion was the only house on the dead-end street, and her mom had already left for work.

Anna quickened her pace, not wanting to be late for her first day at her new school. She focused on the trees ahead, not allowing her gaze to stray to the tombstones on either side of the path. Or to that spooky statue on her right. Or the raven that had just landed on the statue's hand.

Focus.

She never got creeped out like this. Never.

Well, except when she was reading her horror novels.

Or when she stayed up late watching Hitchcock movies. With the lights off. Because she was a risk taker like that. And she loved being scared.

But that was different. That was intentional. And this was . . . this was real life.

Dead people stay dead.

Anna told herself she was being a baby. Winchester Cemetery wasn't *really* haunted, despite the rumors she'd overheard. The girls in line in front of her at the discount store had been so involved in their conversation, they didn't even notice Anna as they talked about the creepy old burial ground next to Mad Manor. "My brother totally saw a ghost there," one of the girls had said. "That place is haunted for sure."

Anna had rolled her eyes. Just stories made up by bored people living in a tiny town.

But a shiver ran down her spine now just the same. She plucked a leaf from her tangled hair and picked up her pace.

Whose great idea was it to take a shortcut through the cemetery anyway? Oh, right. Hers. But she'd been at home in bed with all the lights on when she'd made that decision. It seemed pretty stupid now.

Anna chewed on a fingernail. Her senses were picking up every little detail surrounding her, each setting her more on edge than the one before.

The crunching of her sneakers on loose gravel.

The scent of fresh-cut flowers on the graves.

The light drops of rain.

Her mom hadn't mentioned anything about rain that morning. In fact, she'd told Anna to bring a sweater in case of wind. Anna had listened. She always did. She pulled the thin cardigan closer against her body.

Then her foot hit a rock and she slipped, her wrist grazing the concrete pavement. She could feel the sting immediately, feel the warm blood welling up along her right arm and dripping to the ground. She sat up, ignoring the persistent pain, pulled an old tissue from her worn jeans pocket, and wrapped it snugly around her wrist.

Suddenly the tiny hairs on the back of her neck prickled and an unexplainable surge of panic ran through her. Something wasn't right. That much she knew. She just couldn't explain what it was.

A flash of movement caught her eye from the dark forest ahead. Almost as if someone was running.

Annabel froze at the exact moment someone whispered in her ear.

"Don't move."

The male voice was silky smooth. Anna stood perfectly still, her muscles tensed and her eyes closed tightly. A new shiver ran down her backbone. Her mind began reeling with possible dangers.

"Maybe dealing with you won't be as difficult as I thought," the guy said in that dangerously soft tone. Anna didn't respond—couldn't respond. His footsteps slid over leaves as he circled around until he stood directly in front of her.

She flinched when his warm breath, reeking of garlic and cigarettes, hit her face. She forced her eyes to open. He was tall and lanky, with eyes as gray as the cloudy, miserable day. His face was gaunt, and his hair, wet from the raindrops, was so black that it had a blue tint. A wiry beard traced the sharp angles of his jaw, making him look older than the teenager he no doubt was. He stood perfectly straight, hands clasped behind him.

Instinctively, Anna took a step back.

His lips twisted into a half sneer.

"What do you want?" Anna tried to keep her voice from shaking.

"You have something that belongs to me." His eyes wandered over her before settling on the messenger bag she held tightly against her body.

"Um, I think you've mistaken me for someone else," she said carefully, watching the expression on his face as his eyes flashed.

The rain picked up.

"Annabel," he breathed, venom filling his voice. The

dull rumble of thunder was distant in the sky. "Don't mess with me. Hand it over."

She stared at him, shocked. How did he know her name? She shook her head vigorously, stumbling back in panic and falling over a low headstone. She scrambled to her feet, ignoring the pain, and backed farther away. "No," she said. A bolt of lightning streaked across the sky at the exact moment she turned and ran.

The rain pelted her face as she tore through the graveyard, the guy's footsteps not far behind. The forest loomed closer. Anna had no idea what—or who—lurked inside. But at that moment, it was her best shot. She would take running into an unknown forest over a crazy guy any day.

It was almost pitch black in the woods. Rain dripped from the drenched canopy above her. She zigzagged through the trees, looping around branches and hopping over rocks. Those years of dance classes were definitely paying off.

She pushed through the thick undergrowth and shivered as more rain splattered her. The wind died down as she ran farther and farther into the forest.

Out of breath, Anna slowed to a walk and stopped, turning in a circle. The only sound now was the pounding rain and her own heavy breathing. She didn't think she was still being followed, but she wasn't certain.

Then it hit her.

She was lost in the center of the forest, with no sense of direction. No clue which way was out. And no way of contacting her mom.

Last week Anna had stupidly left her phone in the pocket of her University of Santa Cruz sweatshirt and thrown it in the wash. Of course her mom had chosen to use that occasion to teach her a lesson in responsibility. The only way Anna could get a new phone was to buy it herself.

Anna swallowed her panic. At least she had ditched that creepy guy. And if she didn't show up for school, the Academy would call her mom and she would come looking for her. Eventually.

Up ahead she saw a glimmer of light through the trees. As she inched forward, Anna stumbled over a large root sticking out from an overgrown tree. This had to be a record for the most falls in one day. Her clumsiness had started right around the time her dance class ended, but this was bordering on loser status.

She looked down and a glint of silver caught her eye. She reached under the root and pulled out . . . a phone. It was in a black, scuffed-up case, although the phone itself seemed in good condition. Not a scratch marred its slick surface; no fingerprints smudged the screen.

Anna palmed the phone, turning it over several times. Who would leave this out here? And why?

Suddenly she was overcome with relief. She could call for help!

She punched the power button repeatedly. Nothing happened; the phone remained dark. Dread settled like a rock in the pit of her stomach. The battery was probably dead. Nothing ever went right for her; why would now be any different?

She unzipped the small front pocket on her knock-off black messenger bag and slipped the phone in.

When she reached the edge of the clearing, the light was gone. There was nothing but complete darkness. She pushed a branch out of the way, sending icy water droplets showering down on her skin.

"Nice one, loser," she muttered to herself as she hesitantly stepped into the clearing.

A twig snapped to her right.

Her heart fearfully thrummed in her chest. She took off at a sprint, everything blurring as she ran. Her lungs burned and her legs felt wobbly and weak. Operating on pure adrenaline, she kept going until she found her way out.

CHAPTER 2

ANNA

Anna managed to make it to school ten minutes after the first bell. She didn't even want to think about how bad she looked. That would require a whole other level of brain activity that she wasn't even capable of at the moment.

Anna trudged up to the entrance. Clumps of ivy and tendrilly green plants framed the archway. A bronze plate above the double doors read WINCHESTER ACADEMY. The place looked like some kind of exclusive private school, but it was the public school for all seventh through twelfth graders in Winchester Village.

Anna sighed as she gripped the handle, which was cold and slick from the rain.

"Here goes nothing."

She pushed the heavy door open, the warm air rushing to greet her as she stepped inside. The office was to her right. A tiny blond woman with small black-framed glasses was swallowed up behind a huge mahogany desk. When she saw Anna, she waved her over.

"You must be Annabel. Come in and we'll get you started."

That was both encouraging and dismaying. It was nice to be welcomed so warmly, but if they recognized every one of their students, how big could this school be?

"Hi," Anna said. She took off her soaking sweater and stood holding it awkwardly. The walls were decorated with certificates and plaques showing off just how spectacular this place was. The front office had a welcoming feel to it—leather couches against the walls, a small wood-burning fireplace to her left, and a built-in saltwater aquarium with LED mood lighting right next to the large frosted glass door with the words PRINCIPAL WOODMOORE on it in gold letters. So different from her school back in Sacramento, with its overgrown potted plants and hard plastic chairs in the lobby. But still, it had been *her* school.

Anna couldn't help but feel a little homesick. She reminded herself it was for the best.

"I'm Mrs. Clover." The high-pitched voice matched the secretary perfectly. "It's great to see you're finally here," she said, her eyes flicking to the large wall clock.

"There was this crazy guy at the cemetery. He tried to follow me, and—"

Mrs. Clover waved her off. "I'm not interested in excuses."

Anna nodded, feeling a lump in her throat.

As if just now getting a good look at Anna, Mrs. Clover scrunched her nose and dramatically placed her right hand over her chest. "Oh! You look like a drowned rat."

Annabel shrugged, chewing her bottom lip.

"You might want to get yourself cleaned up before heading to your first class. You're already late, so I doubt another few minutes will matter much."

After Mrs. Clover explained how to get to the girls' room, she gave Anna a schedule along with a crisp laminated map of the school.

"The last three classes of the day are your GATE sessions," she explained.

"GATE?"

"Gifted and Talented Education. Your test score suggests you are at a level above most of your peers." She raised her eyebrows as if she hardly believed it.

Anna had forgotten about the test. Before enrolling her as a student, Winchester Academy had insisted she take a placement exam.

When she'd been handed the test, Anna had drawn a blank. She'd sat at a creaky wooden desk in a room by herself, reading the same questions over and over again, unable to concentrate.

After thirty minutes, the instructor had come back into the room to check on her.

"I'm almost done," Anna had lied. Then she'd panicked and guessed on every question, randomly filling in the multiple-choice bubbles. If Anna hadn't seen the letter of acceptance mailed to her mom, she wouldn't have believed it.

I'm accidentally gifted, Anna thought. *How will I pull this off?*

"Good luck, Annabel." Mrs. Clover gave her a tight-lipped smile, then turned her back, dismissing her as she began riffling through a stack of papers.

In the girls' room, Anna wiped her face with a paper towel and pulled her dull brown hair into a messy bun. She tried to dry her clothes with the hand dryer, but it was useless.

Anna glanced down at her schedule. Her first class

was Language Arts. According to the map, it was on the other side of the building. Great. As if her legs didn't already feel like limp noodles.

The teacher, Mr. Berkin, was a short, stocky man with slicked-back brown hair. He squinted at Anna as she opened the door to the classroom.

"Uh, Annabel?"

She wondered if he asked her that because he wasn't sure of her name or because he couldn't see her properly.

"Yeah." Anna's voice squeaked. She cleared her throat, feeling the heat rush straight to her face.

"Have a seat." He gestured grandly at the desks in front of him, as if he were offering a prize.

Anna headed toward the back, running a critical eye over the dozen students. They were all looking at her with great curiosity. She was willing to bet she was the most interesting thing to happen since the first McDonald's had opened in the tiny town just the month before.

"Hey," she mumbled, giving the class her patented new-girl smile.

A few students murmured back halfheartedly. A girl with vibrant red curly hair that fell in ringlets to her shoulders gave her a friendly wave.

"I'm Millie," she said, glancing at Anna's wet Converse sneakers and ragged-hemmed jeans.

Anna threw her messenger bag down beside the desk and took a seat. "Anna."

Millie had pale skin and blunt bangs that framed wide green eyes and touched the tips of her thick, almost fake-looking lashes. She wore a black rocker tee and leggings.

The teacher went right into the lesson, so there wasn't time to say more. Anna looked down at her desk, feeling everyone's eyes still on her. If there was anything she hated more than fake people, it was being the center of attention.

Mr. Berkin droned on about the book the class was in the middle of reading while Anna replayed the events of the morning. Something outside caught her eye, but it was only the trees swaying in the wind.

Then she noticed the boy two rows over and three seats up. He was absently twirling his pencil and looking out the window. A dark jacket covered his hoodie. Anna's eyes traveled to his shoes. A well-worn pair of dirty Chucks. Maybe she wasn't the only one who didn't really fit in here.

She felt odd staring at him, but she couldn't help it. His dark hair was a bit on the long side, covering one eye when he looked down, and there was something familiar about him. She couldn't put her finger on it, though.

"Hey!" someone whispered. Anna felt a pencil poke her in the arm. It was Millie.

"Huh?"

Millie ripped a page out of her spiral notebook and thrust it at Anna. The paper had scrawled handwriting in blue ink. "Take it," she said, shoving it into Anna's hands.

"Annabel?" Mr. Berkin cleared his throat.

"Um . . ." Anna looked at him like a deer caught in headlights.

He nodded to the paper she still held in her hand. "I'll collect your assignment now."

Anna looked down at the paper, catching a scent of vanilla hand lotion as Millie took it from her and handed it over. He walked away down the aisle, gathering the assignments from the rest of the students. Anna couldn't believe she had spaced out the whole time, not realizing she was supposed to be writing.

Anna turned toward Millie. "Thanks." She hoped her embarrassment wasn't as obvious as it felt.

Millie smiled. "Anytime."

Anna's gaze trailed to her right again. She flinched when she saw *him* staring at her. Well, not staring, but looking. There was a big difference between the two. The sad thing was, boys rarely, if ever, noticed her.

His dark eyes were full of curiosity. She stared

down at her desk, trying to keep her heartbeat at a calm rhythm while still feeling his eyes on her, but when she looked up, he was looking away.

The bell rang and Anna grabbed her bag as the boy glanced up at her, the hint of a smile along his lips. As she walked out of the classroom, she turned around in time to see him walk the opposite way with his friends, but not before he looked back over his shoulder with the same odd smile.

Anna didn't realize she had stopped in the middle of the hallway until some guy ran into her, pushing against her shoulder. "Watch it," he muttered.

"Sorry," she said, tucking a strand of hair behind her ear.

She made her way through the crowded hall toward her next class. Or so she hoped, since she didn't actually know where her next class was.

Welcome to Winchester Academy.

CHAPTER 3

Lucy

Lucy Edwards took time getting ready. She even set her alarm earlier than normal so she could look her absolute best. She had to wear just the perfect, mind-blowing dress; arrange her hair in loose, precise curls; and apply just enough makeup to give her naturally pale complexion a sun-kissed glow. After all, she was in *love*. Not puppy love or an extreme crush. No, this was different. It was the earth-shattering, weak-in-the-knees, stomach-curling type of love that most people would only experience watching a movie. It was a Bella and Edward type of love.

Her stomach did somersaults in anticipation. Today was their anniversary. Their three-week, five-day, four-hour-and . . . two-minute anniversary, as she checked the time on her phone. Not that she was *really* counting.

John was *the* one. Hers forever. For better or worse. Till death did them part. And maybe not even then.

John was meeting her at her house, and they were going to ditch school. Maybe they would take the train and head over to Dover Chase to see a movie.

Where was he? She peered between the slats of her blinds, expecting to see him walk up the road any minute.

Like most girls at Winchester Academy, Lucy didn't worry about money. Unlike most of those same girls, she didn't flaunt her wealth. Well, not as much. And she liked to be generous with what she had.

Lucy impatiently checked the time again, not even enjoying her favorite music reverberating off the sky-blue walls in her bedroom. If he wanted to date her, he would need to learn how seriously she took punctuality.

Maybe she should call him again. Although . . . she

had already called him twelve times this morning, and it might be considered excessive if she called any more. Still, every message she had left him had been for a reason. And it wasn't her fault his voice mail cut her off after only two minutes. She had barely been able to tell him all the plans she had for them today.

But now she knew she *had* to call him at least one more time. She speed-dialed him, hoping he'd have a good explanation. She waited for him to answer, impatiently tapping her foot on the solid oak floor. She couldn't wait till she got her license. Once she could drive, she'd never have to worry about situations like this. Only one year, eleven months, and two weeks to go. And that she *was* counting.

The familiar deep voice sounded in her ear as his voice mail came on. She groaned in frustration, until she heard her name.

"*. . . and if this is Lucy—*"

"Aww, he loves me so much he added me to his new greeting!" she squealed. She danced around the room, not even paying attention to the rest of the message.

"*—seriously, stop calling. And don't even think about leaving another message.*" BEEEP.

"Hey, John, it's okay you're late. I just hope you're on your way. I totally forgive you! Smooches!"

She hung up, flinging herself onto the oversized

plush sofa in the corner of her room, with ten pillows too many, not even noticing the wrinkles she was putting in her beige raw-silk skirt.

All Lucy could hear was her joyful, racing heart beating in tune to her favorite song. She cranked up her speakers, singing along to Beyoncé. And for the first time, she didn't even care that she sounded like a strangled cat.

CHAPTER 4

ΛΝΝΛ

Anna had been at school for only three hours and already she had heard four—make that five—rumors going around about her:

1. She'd moved from the fabulous Hollywood Hills.
2. Where her mom used to be a stylist to the stars.
3. But city life was draining, and Winchester Village had the perfect quiet life they needed.
4. So they'd packed up their Beamer.
5. And begun their new exciting life in their upscale, three-story lakeside home.

Nobody batted an eye when details changed in certain versions. Anna didn't bother correcting them. They could think whatever they wanted about her . . . especially since the rumors made her sound so much more interesting. Besides, they made it easier for her to hide the truth.

At the Academy, the gym served as the cafeteria, although some students preferred to hang out by their lockers or lounge on the benches in hallways or under the trees in the courtyard. The upper grades could go off campus.

Millie sat with Anna on one of the benches at the end of a hallway, a bottle of Vitamin Water next to her, untouched. Anna had her favorite sack lunch—grilled cheese and pesto sandwich, sliced apple with no peel, and water. Maybe tomorrow she'd be daring and buy lunch.

Anna took a bite of her sandwich, checking out her new classmates. In spite of how small the school was, it still had the usual cliques: jocks, nerds, goths, populars. It also had the not-so-usual cliques: the snooty, the rich, the even richer, the fashionable, and all of the above.

Suddenly the loud voices and laughter died to a low murmur. Hushed whispers filled the hallway.

That was when *they* appeared.

A group of five girls glided down the corridor in their four-inch platforms, tiny pink skirts, and pink silky tops. They took no notice of the group of guys who said hi as they passed, or the two girls sitting up against the lockers who could easily see up their short skirts as they walked by. The group seemed to have their sights on one thing and one thing only, and they homed in on it like heat-seeking missiles: Annabel.

Anna did a double take. Each one of them was tall and thin, with perfect porcelain skin and hair so blond it was nearly white.

Anna found herself being sucked into their presence as if they were A-list celebrities. She stared at them, the bite of sandwich in her mouth going unchewed as her jaw dropped slightly.

She wondered how people could tell the girls apart. The only ones who were obviously different were the two identical twins leading the group.

Millie nudged Anna. "They're coming for you."

"What?" Anna turned to Millie.

Millie gave her a wide-eyed look of warning. "The Ashbury twins. Olivia's the one with all the power. She's on the left. Eden's on the right. And their clones. You'll see."

Anna chuckled. "Okay then."

No sooner had Annabel turned around than the

group stood in front of her, in all their pink glory. They stood confidently, shoulders back, chests out, sizing Anna up in an uncomfortable silence, not even acknowledging Millie. Anna gazed back coolly, hoping she looked more confident than she felt.

"Hi, Annabel," Olivia Ashbury said.

"Anna," she corrected the twin.

Olivia shrugged. "Whatever."

Anna's eyes darted over the girls in the group, and she bit back a smile. Did they realize how ridiculously *pink* they looked? Why would they want to look so freakishly alike?

Eden stood slightly behind her sister, glancing at Anna's sneakers.

"So, Annabel," said Olivia. "We're going to the Corner Café after school."

Anna raised an eyebrow.

"The coffee shop down the street?" Olivia prompted.

Millie rolled her eyes.

"Yeah, sure," Anna said. She wondered what was up with the invisible treatment they were giving Millie.

Olivia kept a tight-lipped smile. "So we'll see you there after school, then."

"Um . . . okay." They were actually inviting *her*? Anna felt like she was being set up for a prank.

"That place isn't so hot," Millie mumbled.

Olivia snapped her fingers and held her hand out, signaling to her sister/personal assistant. Eden placed a small silver compact in Olivia's hand. Olivia took out a slender tube and applied a fresh coat of pink lip gloss to her lips. "Try to control your excitement," she said to Anna, then snapped the lid closed, arching one perfect pale eyebrow.

Eden walked forward and bent over, placing her warm hand on top of Anna's. "Annabel, consider this a one-time invitation."

Anna was pretty sure nobody ever turned down the Ashbury twins.

Tossing their silky straight hair, the Ashbury twins turned and gracefully walked away, the rest of the girls following closely.

"Um, that was weird." Anna turned to Millie. "How do they even know who I am?"

Millie's eyes flickered with something—jealousy? envy?—before she broke into a toothy grin. "You're fresh meat. *Everyone* knows who you are."

"Everyone?" Her heart sank. Did they all know she lived in creepy Mad Manor? That her backyard consisted of ten thousand dead people? And that she was poor, a word none of these kids used—ever? Or, worst of all, did they know that crazy Maxwell Maddsen had been her great-uncle?

Anna wanted to be normal. She would even settle for being a wallflower. She had hoped she could make a few friends. But if everyone knew about her already, then they knew how un-normal she really was. She would be the freaky new girl at Winchester Academy.

"Well, yeah," said Millie. "Everyone was expecting the new student today. People are making a point to walk past you or accidentally run into you in the hallways."

"Oh." Anna let out a huge sigh, her shoulders slumping forward. "So, where exactly is the Corner Café?"

Millie's eyes widened. "You're not seriously thinking about going."

Anna shrugged. "Why not?" She hoped she appeared cool, when on the inside she was doing the happiest happy dance she'd done in a long time.

"Those *girls*," Millie said, pointing a finger down the hallway, "are cheating, boyfriend-stealing gossip lovers."

And popular, Anna silently added.

"Hey," said Millie, changing her tone. "We should go to Dover Chase sometime. That town has everything—a mall and a movie theater!"

Anna looked up at Millie. Her cheeks were tinged with pink, and there was a hopeful gleam in her eyes.

"Okay. Sure. And I want to buy some hand lotion." Maybe vanilla scented, like Millie's.

Millie smiled. "Cool! I'll text you later." She grabbed her phone, pulling up the contacts list. "What's your number?"

Anna bit her bottom lip, slightly embarrassed. She had no idea how long it would take to save up for a new phone—possibly forever—since her mom had had the brilliant idea that Anna could get the money by finding odd jobs around town. Yeah, fat chance.

"I don't have one. Well, not right now, I mean."

Millie stared at her. "Seriously?"

"Well, I had one. But it got messed up and my mom won't buy me a new one."

"I could never survive without mine. It's like my lifeline."

"Yeah," Anna sighed. "I know."

Millie squinted. "Uh, isn't *that* a phone?"

Anna followed Millie's gaze and looked down at the phone she'd found in the woods. It was sticking out the front pocket of her messenger bag. Frowning, she pulled it out and shook her head. "This? No, I just found it this morning. It's a little beat up and the battery's dead. You don't know anyone who lost a phone, do you?"

"Nope." Millie grinned at her. "But if you can get it to work, maybe today's your lucky day."

Anna smiled back. "I hope you're right." Anna wasn't used to having lucky days. But maybe, just maybe, her luck was about to change.

CHAPTER 5

ANNA

Once the final bell rang, Anna rearranged her artfully messy bun and put on some strawberry lip gloss. And then she headed straight for the Corner Café.

As she pushed open the door, she was surprised to hear someone call her name. "Anna?"

She turned and stared into a pair of the brightest blue eyes she'd ever seen. It was *him*. The boy from her English class. And her history class, although she'd sat in the very back and he hadn't seemed to notice her at all. And he knew her name.

Her breath caught and she felt her cheeks turn pink.

"I'm Johnny. Olivia said you were meeting her here." A dimple creased the right corner of his mouth, making his smile contagious. "She wanted me to let you know she'll be here in a few minutes. She had to run back to her locker and grab her books."

"Uh, yeah. Hi," Anna said, attempting to recover. "Yeah. Olivia." Could she possibly be any more of a dork? He was going to think she didn't know how to speak in complete sentences.

Johnny looked around. "Eden might already be here."

Anna nodded. Right. Olivia. Johnny had a girlfriend. Of course he had a girlfriend. And of course it was one of the Ashbury twins. She felt a surge of disappointment but immediately pushed it away. She didn't want a boyfriend anyway. She was just trying to fit in and make friends.

They stood for a few moments in silence, watching students pass the window. Anna felt awkward and gawky standing next to Johnny. He was at least a head taller, and his shoulders were broad and muscular. He was wearing a football jersey. She looked at him from the corner of her eye as he scanned the crowd.

"There she is." Johnny motioned toward Olivia, who was walking toward them, her heels clacking.

She definitely has confidence, Anna thought. "Hey," she said as Olivia approached.

Johnny whispered something to Olivia and she giggled. Anna self-consciously touched her hair. Her jeans and top were fine but nothing special. She'd purposely tried to dress as casually as possible this morning—she didn't want to look like she was trying too hard. And her still-damp sweater was balled up in her bag. Olivia, on the other hand, wore makeup that looked almost professionally done, a miniskirt, and a pink lacy tank top that fit her perfectly.

"So." Olivia put on big sunglasses that hid her eyes. "I saw the rest of the group with their books at a table on the other side. We should head over."

Books? That took Anna by surprise. Olivia and her crew didn't seem like the type to sit around and study. But maybe things were just different like that in a small town.

"Gotta get to practice. See you guys later." Johnny headed off in the opposite direction, leaving Anna alone with Olivia. She could almost feel Olivia's cold eyes boring into her through her dark glasses before she turned without a word and led Anna across the room.

Eden's face lit up as Anna pulled out a chair next to her.

"Hey, Annabel!"

"Hi." Anna's eyes shifted to Olivia, who seemed to be scowling at her. She definitely got the impression Olivia didn't want her around. Which made no sense at all, since she was the one who'd invited her in the first place.

Sitting next to Eden was one of the clones from the hallway.

"This is Nessa Bloom," Eden said. Nessa glanced up from her textbook only long enough to give Anna a slight nod.

Everyone except Anna began opening their textbooks and notebooks and grabbing their pens. She silently watched them, trying to figure it out.

"So, Anna." Olivia looked down at her through her sunglasses. "You're in GATE, right?"

"Um . . ." For a moment she didn't know what Olivia was talking about. Then she remembered. The gifted program. "Yeah. Are you?" Did they know she was a fake? A total gifted fluke?

Olivia tilted her head back and laughed. "God, no."

"So how did you know?"

"Nothing is secret around here. Get used to it." Olivia slid over her textbook. "I'm sure a genius like you will be able to do these problems fast."

Anna stared at the textbook. "Problems?"

"Yeah. For algebra." She took the paperback Eden was holding and tossed it to Anna. "And you've probably read the first thirty pages of this already. Or even the entire thing. So whatever, just take notes on the first three chapters. Here's my notebook."

"You want me to do your assignments for you?" If

Anna's jaw hadn't been attached, her chin would've landed on the table at that exact moment.

Silence.

Olivia frowned. "Of course not. You're just contributing to the study group."

Study group? Is that why I was invited?

"You do want to be a part of the group, right?" Eden asked.

"Well . . ." Anna wasn't so sure.

"It's totally up to you," Eden said coolly. "No pressure."

"I'll even make it easy for you," Olivia explained. "Meet me in the girls' room before school and I'll take the finished assignments from you."

"The girls' room?" Anna repeated.

"You don't want anyone to see you giving me the homework," Olivia said in a tone most people reserved for preschoolers. "That could make you look bad, right?"

Anna nodded slowly. "Yeah. Right."

"Hey." Olivia elbowed Eden. "Check it out."

Anna followed their gaze to a table behind her. A girl had her nose in a book, literally. It covered most of her face.

"Hey, weirdo!" Olivia called, laughing.

The girl didn't acknowledge her, but her eyebrows arched slightly.

"C'mon, Liv," Eden muttered.

"What, you think she cares? Obviously she dresses like that because she wants attention. So I'm giving her what she wants."

Anna hadn't even noticed her clothes. The girl had on black lace-up boots, purple leggings, and a green skirt. Maybe the girl was color-blind. Or dressed herself in the dark.

"Who is that?" Anna asked. It came out as more of a whisper.

Olivia waved her hand dismissively. "That's nobody."

Eden leaned toward Anna. "Her name is Lucy Edwards. She's a little strange, but she doesn't bother anyone."

"You know that's not true," Olivia said with a smirk. "And if she doesn't back off, I'll have to make her." She made a point of speaking loudly enough for anyone to hear.

"Yeah, you're so scary!" Eden laughed. She turned her attention to Anna. "Don't mind her, she's all bark. So listen, I'm having a party on Friday—"

"Eden!" Olivia glared at her sister.

"Sorry." Eden turned back to Anna. "*We're* having a party."

Olivia shook her head.

"And," continued Eden, "it will be fabulous, as

always." Her eyes grew big as she gestured animatedly with her hands. "We have one to kick off every school year. You know, just to have fun and unwind."

"That sounds great." Anna could hardly believe her ears. Was Eden really inviting her?

"Well," Olivia chimed in, casting a quick glance in Eden's direction, "we don't really have the guest list finalized—"

"—but you should totally come," Eden finished the sentence.

"Their parties are always a blast." Nessa smiled, revealing a row of perfectly straight, too-white teeth. Probably veneers. "Ouch!" Nessa exclaimed as Olivia kicked her under the table.

"Of course, we understand if you have other plans." Olivia placed her chin in her hands, raising one perfectly shaped pale brow.

"Um . . ." Anna felt indecisive. If she said she could go to the party, she'd definitely have to be part of their "study group." But doing Olivia's homework was a small price to pay if it meant she'd be accepted at her new school. And going to their party sounded like a definite popularity booster.

"A party sounds great," Anna said, breaking the uneasy silence. "And I—I'd like to be in your, uh, study group."

"Super," Olivia said breezily. "Give me your cell."

She held her hand out to Anna. "I'll give you my number and you can text me later for the party deets."

This no-phone thing was going to haunt her forever.

"I don't have a phone. I mean, mine broke, but I'm getting a new one. Soon."

Olivia looked at her, horrified. "You don't have a phone? Really?"

"Really." Anna looked down at the table.

"That's okay," Eden said. "I'll meet up with you before then and give you the info."

Anna began shoving the books in her bag. "My mom's forcing me to help with unpacking stuff. She'll throw a fit if I'm too late."

"No prob," Olivia said as Nessa whispered something in her ear and they both laughed. She tilted her chin at Anna. "Make me look smart."

"Sure. Okay," Anna said, pushing in her chair and giving a small wave as she walked out. She knew how pathetic this was. But she couldn't deny it: she was excited. After all, this was the first time she had ever received an invitation to a real party.

CHAPTER 6

ANNA

Anna tossed her messenger bag onto her bed. The old black iron bed frame took up most of the space in her new room, but Anna liked its Gothic look. She had chosen this room for two reasons:

1. The walls were painted a deep purple—her favorite color—so she had instantly been drawn to it.
2. It was a corner room on the third floor, with high, slanted ceilings that reminded her of

a tower room in a Disney movie. It almost inspired her to attempt to grow out her hair.

She kept her room simple: a dresser with a mirror, a black bedside table, and a matching desk. Once she finished unpacking, she could worry about decorating the walls. It might not have been a perfect space, but it was all hers. And that was something she'd never had before.

After shutting her bedroom door, she walked over to her bag and began pulling out the books, stacking them in a neat pile on the desk next to a book her mom had bought her a few weeks ago that she hadn't had a chance to read yet. She felt torn, unsure whether she should actually do all this homework that wasn't hers. But at the same time, she didn't want to be uninvited to the party. And maybe she only needed to do it this once. Maybe they were testing her.

Anna jumped as vibrating from her bag caught her attention. She rifled through the contents, looking for the source, and felt it coming from the front pocket. She unzipped the pouch, pulling out the phone she had found earlier that morning.

She stared at the screen, lit up with an incoming text message. What the heck? Hadn't the phone been dead? She had tried to get the thing to work and it was useless. But then again, she'd been in a bit of a hurry. Maybe she hadn't held the power button down long enough. Or maybe she'd held it too long. Or . . .

Or maybe it had just enough charge to power back on.

Anna shrugged. What did she care? It was actually working now, and that was what mattered.

She punched the button, reading the text message and blowing out a huge sigh.

Help.

That was the entire message. No name or anything to ID the number that popped up. She typed:

Sorry, not my phone. Found it. Do you know who it belongs to? And hit reply.

Anna tried using the other features on the phone—contacts, photos, camera. But when she pushed the buttons, nothing happened. The phone remained frozen on the text message.

Anna pushed the reply button again: still nothing.

She hit delete.

The message remained.

The phone was frozen. Or broken.

"Why do you have to stop working again?" she muttered as she flung it onto her purple pillowcase.

"Who are you talking to?" Valerie Craven walked in, cradling a stack of boxes up to her neck. She gave her daughter a quick glance before setting them down on the hardwood floor against the wall.

"Just myself." Anna sat on top of the phone, hiding it.

Her mother rubbed her hands together. "Aren't you cold, kiddo? I can turn up the heat. Seems this room is a little draftier than the others."

Anna shrugged. "Yeah, sure."

Her mom offered a smile, although it didn't quite reach her eyes. "How was school?"

"Good." Anna hesitated. Should she tell her about the encounter with the creepy guy? Maybe her mom had seen him when she was driving to work this morning. "Actually, have you seen a weird skinny guy hanging around the cemetery?"

"Weird like how?" her mom asked, looking at her with the overly concerned expression that only moms can master.

Anna knew something like this would really worry her mom, who was already stressed and exhausted from the move. And she'd been putting in extra hours at Twisted, a popular salon in town. Anna decided she probably shouldn't bother her with this right now.

She shrugged. "I dunno. There was just this guy I saw on my way to school today. He was outside even in the rain. . . ." She trailed off, purposely leaving out the details.

A relieved look spread across her mother's face. "Oh, it was probably just someone visiting one of the graves. Grief can do many things to a person. It seems pretty safe here, although I'm sure they have their share of oddballs."

Anna raised her eyebrows.

"Small towns aren't like the city. Everyone knows everyone else's business, and gossip spreads faster than fire."

"That is so cliché, Mom."

"You know what I mean. And I'm sure you'll hear rumors about your great-uncle Maxwell, especially since we're living in his old house."

"Rumors? Like what?" Anna asked. She had no plans to tell anyone where she lived.

"Nothing you need to worry about."

"C'mon, Mom. You know I'll eventually hear about it."

Anna's mom always wanted to protect her from everything, especially since she was an only child. But at the same time, they usually were able to talk about anything.

"Well, my uncle Maxwell claimed he was haunted by voices. And he saw things that weren't actually there. Your great-aunt Esther tried her whole life to get him help, but he refused. It actually offended him that anyone could think he was crazy. Some people in town say it was old age. . . ." She shook her head, her voice trailing off. "But I knew him when he wasn't that old."

"And that's why you kept me away from him?"

Her mom nodded. "I didn't want to put you in a situation like that. It was for the best."

Anna looked down at her feet, playing with the string on her hoodie. She always felt a bit uncomfortable when her mom looked so sad. Like when Anna asked questions about her dad. He had died when she was too young to even remember him. Her mom always shook her head, her eyes glossy with unshed tears, and brushed her off with "When you're older."

But Anna was thirteen. An eighth grader—practically in high school. She *was* older. How long would it take for her mom to realize that?

"Didn't you say Maxwell died from a heart attack?" Anna asked.

Her mom nodded. "Technically. But who knows? He was seventy years old. Maybe it was a lifetime of other things that drove him to his grave."

"Since I'm related to him, doesn't that mean I have a

chance of . . . you know . . . becoming like that too?" Her mom seemed fine, but maybe it skipped generations.

"Of course not. He had a hard life, and sometimes people don't deal well with difficult situations." Her mom pointed to the boxes. "So, can you get around to unpacking these?"

"Yeah, after my homework."

Her mom did a double take as she spotted the books crowding Anna's desk. "Don't you have a locker for all those? They look heavy."

"I didn't have time to find it today. I barely made it to all my classes in time."

Her mom laughed. "You'll get used to it. Did you get all the classes you wanted?"

Anna shrugged. "They're all pretty much the same ones I had at my old school. Except now I'm gifted. And gifted is code for three times the homework."

Anna's mom gave her a hug. "Well, I'm proud of you. And don't forget, we're still going out to dinner to celebrate."

Anna blew out a huge sigh. Her mom would be so disappointed if she knew what a phony she really was. She was surprised her mom hadn't already framed the letter announcing her acceptance into the GATE program.

"And if the classes really are too hard, I'll talk to the school. I'll be downstairs if you need me."

"That narrows it down," Anna said. The Manor was so large it practically had its own zip code. What she really needed was a map. "Okay, I'll text you if I need you." She smacked the side of her head. "Oh, wait, I forgot, I don't have a phone."

Her mom pointed a finger at her. "You should post an ad at the Club House offering your fantastic baby-sitting services," she suggested. "I bet you could save up money in no time."

The Winchester Club House was the town's pool club. Everyone who lived in Winchester had access. There were two swimming pools, one with a miniature waterfall and a twist slide; tennis courts; basketball courts; and a clubhouse with a gym, a screening room, and everything from air hockey to pool tables. It was a popular place for the families in town to gather on weekends and have a BBQ, and sometimes it would be rented out for parties. But most of the time it was just somewhere to hang out.

"Or you could just buy me a new one," Anna tried.

"We've been over this before. If you want a new phone, you'll have to pay for it. And then maybe you'll learn how to take care of your things."

"Whatever." Anna rolled her eyes as her mom left the room.

She lay back on her bed. She had no idea how she

would get all her own homework done tonight, let alone everyone else's.

A soft buzz sounded near Anna's ear. She rolled onto her side and plucked the phone off her pillow.

2 new text messages

"What the heck?" she muttered. She looked at the new messages.

> **I said I need help.**
> **Why won't you help me?**

Anna hit reply. And this time it worked.

> **Who are you trying to reach?**

Not even a second later, the screen flashed with one word:

> **YOU**

Obviously this person didn't understand. Although how Anna could be any clearer, she had no idea. Still, she typed back:

> **Look, I found this phone. It's not even mine!**

The phone died once again, turning off.

Anna shook her head. She pushed the power button at the top of the phone, and unsurprisingly, nothing happened.

"Of course you only work when you want to," Anna grumbled. She hid the phone in the top drawer of her nightstand.

A train whistle blew in the distance. Anna swung her legs over the side of her bed and turned on her bedside lamp, then stood and walked over to her window. She looked outside, down at the sidewalk. The sun was setting, casting shadows, playing tricks with her mind. Two squirrels chased each other up a tree. Something else moved, catching her eye. Someone was leaning against one of the crooked old oak trees, a guy with his hands shoved deep in the pockets of his jeans. At least, she assumed it was a guy, from the broad shoulders and the way he was standing. His hood covered most of his hair, but she could still tell it was dark.

Her heart thumped in her throat.

A loud buzzing sounded from her top drawer.

Anna flinched for a moment, her gaze flicking down to her nightstand. Her skin prickled. She quickly looked out the window again.

He was gone.

Her eyes searched the area surrounding her house, but she saw no one. She stared at the last place she'd seen the guy, but the only evidence anyone had even been there was the leaves blowing across the bricks like a soft breeze had stirred them.

Could it be someone from school? She quickly shook the thought away. There was no way anyone could know where she lived yet. The other possibilities creeped her out more than a little. Like the awful guy from the cemetery. She thought how he could have easily guessed where she lived, especially if he'd seen her walking out her back gate that morning.

Her heart hammered as she left her room and went down the spiral staircase to the first floor, her stomach growling the whole way.

The soft glow from the lamps and flickering cinnamon candles made the house feel warmer than it had earlier in the day and smell more comforting, like home. But Anna couldn't push back the paranoia she felt. As she came to the bottom floor, her eyes darted toward the front door and she had an urge to look out.

She shook her head and turned down the hall. Several boxes sat on the sofa in the living room, and handfuls of wrinkled newspaper covered the glass center of the coffee table. The tan walls were chipped and beginning to crack, and an outdated wallpaper border was at risk of peeling off.

Over the past week she'd noticed that there were

exactly twelve clocks throughout the house. Old, ugly clocks that didn't make a sound, not a single tick. The hands were frozen at midnight. On every single one.

She made her way to the kitchen, grabbing a snack of cheese and crackers before heading back up to the third floor. She cringed with each creak the steps made. Halfway up, she saw a shadow out of the corner of her eye.

Annabel froze midstep as she caught a woody scent lingering in the air. Tobacco smoke? It reminded her of the smell in the old library downstairs. A shiver curled the hairs on the back of her neck, cascading down her backbone. It took everything in her to not hurl herself back down the stairs toward the front door.

She pushed herself forward, and the first thing she noticed when she reached her room was the darkness. She could've sworn she'd left her light on.

Anna slowly shuffled with arms out in front of her as she felt around for her lamp, trying to avoid bumping into the bed. She clicked it on and the light illuminated her cozy purple-walled room. The schoolbooks still sat untouched on her desk, but she didn't open them.

Instead, she went to the window and looked down in the yard.

Nobody was there. Anna couldn't help but wonder if maybe she had imagined it all.

A loud thump brought her attention back to her desk.

One of the old books from the library, a collection of poems by Edgar Allan Poe, lay on the ground, wide open.

Her eyes fell on the black, bold letters of a poem. "Annabel Lee," on page 121.

A black circular mark that looked like it was from a cigarette marred the bottom of the page across from it, right beside the last two lines of another poem, "A Dream Within a Dream."

> *Is all that we see or seem*
> *But a dream within a dream?*

CHAPTER 7

Lucy

That same night, Lucy flung herself across her bed. How could he stand her up like that? And today of all days. She plucked a chocolate from the emergency box stashed in her nightstand, second drawer from the bottom.

"I just don't get it," she grumbled, popping a hazelnut truffle into her mouth.

Outside, the setting sun created a swirl of colors like a painter's palette. The shadows danced across her room, a reminder that another day was ending, another day that her phone didn't ring and she still hadn't heard from John. Lucy got up and slapped the blinds closed. She wasn't in the mood for anything beautiful.

Sitting on the edge of her bed, she reached for a chocolate covered with sprinkles. Maybe, she thought, he hadn't stood her up. Maybe he was sick. Or something had happened, something extreme, something that had prevented him from making it to her house. Or to his phone to call her.

A wave of worry washed over her. The possibilities whirled through her mind. What kind of a girlfriend was she? The kind who sat around eating high-calorie candies while wallowing in self-pity?

No. She stood up. "I'm the kind of girlfriend who is always there for my boyfriend," she whispered. She carefully placed the half-eaten chocolate back into its wrapper, saving it for later, and closed the lid on the box. Now she just needed to figure out where to find him.

With her phone in hand, Lucy marched downstairs and out the front door. She pulled up her flashlight app and headed down the street toward his house—or rather, where she thought his house was. Because actually, she had never had the chance to visit him. Yet. But she had seen him walk in that direction one time after school.

Lucy's chunky black heels crunched on the gravel road, the tiny beam of light from her phone flittering back and forth on the ground in front of her. Her feet were already killing her. Being fashionable was a lot of work.

An owl called nearby. Frogs croaked. Crickets chirped. The small sounds were unnerving, breaking the silence. She didn't want to be left alone with her thoughts. She needed a distraction. She needed to set the mood.

She popped her earbuds in and scrolled through her playlist, selecting the one titled "All Things John." She had put that together the day he had given her his phone number. Since then, she continually added songs that reminded her of him to the quickly growing list. She adjusted the volume, turning up "Forever and Always" by Taylor Swift, the song she'd wasted no time adding when John was a no-show.

A new text flashed across the screen. Was it him?

She pulled up the message, sighing. It was only her mom. Probably saying she was staying for another week in New York for business. She definitely had bad timing and a habit of being highly annoying at the worst possible moments.

Another text came in before she had a chance to read the first one.

If she had been coordinated, she would've jumped up and down at that exact second. But she didn't trust herself to pull it off, especially wearing heels.

Opting for balance, Lucy slowed her pace, frowning, as she read the message.

8 pm Winchester Cemetery. Friday night.
Surprise. Don't text back.

What did John mean, don't text back? Telling her not to do something only made her want to do it ten times more. But instead, she practiced her patience, closed her eyes, and counted to eleven and a half. Then she took a long, deep breath and opened her eyes. There. All better.

Friday night was only four days away. What would she wear? How would she do her hair? Lucy came to a dead stop. "But . . . why does he want to meet in the graveyard?" she mumbled. She put the phone next to her heart. Maybe it symbolized something. Something fantastic. Something like . . . his undying love for her.

Lucy spun herself around and teetered back toward her house. She didn't have to go look for John. He had come to her without her even trying.

CHAPTER 8

ANNA

There was a bite to the air, and Anna could almost make out the fog from her breath as she walked to school. She'd gotten only a few hours of sleep, thanks to bad dreams. And on top of that, she'd had to wake up even earlier to avoid taking the dreaded shortcut through the cemetery.

All the creepy noises Anna had heard the night before replayed in her exhausted brain. The footsteps on the stairs, creaking doors, the scraping of branches on her bedroom window like fingernails raking along the glass. She'd woken up with her bedroom window wide open. Why her mom would open it she had no idea. It was more than a little strange, since her mom knew her room was colder than the others in the house.

Only a few students were outside the school, but they were rushing indoors. Except one person, who sat on the steps dressed in a T-shirt and leggings, head in hands.

As Anna got closer, she realized that it was Millie.

"Hey!" Millie waved, looking way too cheerful so early on a Tuesday morning.

"Hey," Anna said. "Aren't you cold?" She'd worn her white denim jacket over a long-sleeve tee, and even that wasn't warm enough.

Millie shook her head. "Nah, I'm used to it." She stood up and walked inside with Anna. "So, did you meet up with *them* after school yesterday?"

Anna shrugged. She didn't really want to tell Millie what had happened. It was obvious Olivia was using her, but she wasn't going to admit that to anyone. Still, Anna wanted to make friends, and it was hard enough keeping secrets without having to lie on top of it.

"Yeah, for a little while. It wasn't *that* bad." She didn't bring up the party in case Millie wasn't invited.

Millie raised an eyebrow.

"Well, okay. Maybe you were right about Olivia and she is a bit . . . rude. But Eden seems cool. I might even join their study group."

Millie snickered. "Yeah, right. Like they ever study. They probably only get passing grades because someone does their work for them."

"I wouldn't be surprised," Anna muttered. She shifted her messenger bag to her other shoulder. "So . . . I'll see you later, okay?" And before Millie could say anything, Anna took off. Her shoulders ached and the strap of her bag was digging into her skin, even through her coat. She walked down the hallways, searching the numbers on the lockers for the one she had been assigned.

As she passed other students, she noticed a few nearby whispering. She caught the words "new girl" more than once. Anna tried to look oblivious.

To her relief, she found her locker pretty quickly. Locker 121.

She stared at the number for a minute, not sure why it sounded so familiar. She twisted the combination as given on the paper she held in her hand and tried the locker.

She pulled harder. It didn't open. She tried the combination again. It still didn't open. She groaned, leaning her head against the locker, and silently prayed for it to open.

"Need some help?"

Anna snapped her head up. A guy with large black glasses and a monstrous camera hanging around his neck was grinning at her.

She held back a laugh. This was how her prayer was answered?

She threw up her hands in defeat. "I can't get my locker open."

"I noticed," he said. When Anna stared blankly at him, he laughed. "Want me to try?"

"Okay," Anna said, offering him the paper with the combination.

"Sure," he said. He gave her a sideways glance. "Aren't you afraid of giving your locker combo to a complete stranger? You never know what I might do with it."

"Well, I can't open it, so right now there's nothing even in it," Anna said.

He twisted and turned the dial expertly. The locker opened.

"How did you do that?" Anna demanded, amazed.

"Years of experience." He tipped an imaginary hat and headed down the hallway.

"Hey, what's your name?" Anna called after him, realizing she should have been friendlier.

He looked back at her, dark eyebrows raised. "Spencer."

"Thanks, Spencer!"

He nodded and a moment later he disappeared into the crowd of students. Anna looked into her empty open locker and threw her books in mechanically, coming across the phone and hesitating for a moment before placing it back in her bag. She had grabbed the phone that morning, even though its screen remained dark, because she didn't want to take the chance that it would suddenly decide to come back to life while she was at school and her mom would find it.

In Language Arts, Anna glanced around for an empty seat. Millie mouthed "Sorry" to her, since someone had already taken hers from yesterday. Some students were standing around, talking to their friends, their backpacks thrown on top of nearby desks claiming their seats. Toward the back she saw two adjacent empty seats behind two guys fist-bumping.

She started making her way, watching her feet, but when she looked up again, there was only one seat left. Johnny sat in the other. He was wearing the same jacket as the day before—it looked a bit beaten up and could probably have used a wash—with a forest-green hoodie underneath.

As she plopped her bag on the ground next to her desk, Anna reminded herself to breathe and act normal. Johnny didn't spare a glance at her, even after she sat down next to him.

Maybe he didn't remember her from yesterday. Maybe he had a short-term memory problem.

The classroom door opened and closed for the next few minutes as more students trailed in. Without moving her head, Anna stole a look at Johnny as he nervously ran a hand through his shaggy dark hair.

Then he finally tilted his head toward her.

"So, how you like it here?" he asked.

So maybe his memory wasn't so short-term after all.

"Good. I like it . . ." She trailed off because she didn't know what else to say. She picked up her pencil and doodled a cupcake on her notebook. *C'mon, Anna. Say something.*

"So . . ." He paused for a moment, clearing his throat, and out of the corner of her eye she could see one of the girls with ice-blond hair taking an overly obvious interest in her. She thought it was Nessa. She was probably spying so she could report everything back to Olivia. "Where do you live?"

"Oh. Um." She didn't want to lie, but she definitely didn't want to tell him the truth. "Not too far from here. How about you?"

A smile crept across his face. "I'm not too far away either."

Anna giggled nervously. At least he didn't ask her anything else.

The teacher walked down the aisle between the two of them as he handed back graded quizzes from the week before.

Anna still had the feeling there was something about Johnny that was so . . . familiar. She couldn't quite figure out why, though.

When class was over, Anna followed the rest of the students pushing their way out. Millie had already disappeared.

At lunchtime, Anna didn't see Millie anywhere in the halls or at the bench where they'd eaten the day before, so she walked into the cafeteria alone and stared dismally out over the crowds of students laughing, gossiping, and eating at their tables. She spotted Spencer leaning against the milk cooler, talking to the guy in front of him in the lunch line, juggling a bottle of water and laughing.

Anna grabbed a water bottle to put on her tray, watching as Spencer reached for his camera and started taking pictures of the students around him. Missing her tray completely, she dropped the water bottle, which crashed to the ground and bounced against the leg of the girl in front of her. With an aggravated sigh, the girl spun around to face Anna, attitude written on her face.

"Way to go, new girl!" she snapped.

"Sorry," Anna apologized, flushing. "It was an accident."

The commotion caused other people in line to look over at her, including Spencer and his camera. Anna quickly looked down, covering her face with her mousy brown hair just as a flash went off in her direction.

Just great, Anna thought. She passed up the frozen pizza that was seared under the heating lamps and "chicken patties" topped with shriveled lettuce and grabbed the only edible-looking thing, an apple. Impulsively she put a granola bar on the tray too.

After she paid for her food, she hesitated. Should she sit with a group of people she didn't know or sit by herself at one of the few empty tables in the cafeteria?

She couldn't just stand there. She would look like a total loser. Trying to look confident, she quickly walked to the nearest crowded table, with only one empty seat, plunking her tray down in front of her as she sat.

Like they were in a scene in a bad movie, everyone at the table stopped talking and turned to stare at her. The silence lengthened uncomfortably, and Anna wasn't sure what to do. So she stared down at her food and then looked back up at the group around her. They were still just looking at her. Anna felt her cheeks burn pink.

"What's up, new girl?" a girl with a black pixie cut said at last.

"Hey," Anna replied. It came out as such a whisper, she wasn't even sure she'd said the word aloud.

"Where'd you move from?" a thin boy with unruly hair asked.

"Sacramento." She figured she should set the rumors straight before they got too out of control.

A girl named Claire who she recognized from gym class put her hand on Anna's arm in a comforting gesture. "That is so tragic."

"It is?" Anna couldn't help it; the question just fell out of her mouth.

"Did you live close to a mall?" a girl in a gray lace crop top asked. "That's my dream."

"Kind of. Sacramento has a lot of malls. It's a big city." Anna's voice cracked.

And just as quickly as the questions began, they stopped, and the awkward silence returned.

This had been a big mistake. She stood up abruptly. "Actually, I see someone I know. Nice to meet you guys." She quickly walked away from the table. "Never, ever do that again," she muttered under her breath.

Spotting an empty table in the very back near the fire exit, Anna made a beeline for it. No sooner did she sit down than a girl with a lunch tray walked straight toward her.

The girl, who looked super familiar to Anna, was bouncy—a little too excited to be in school. Anna's eyes fell immediately on her boots. The heels had to be at least three inches, and even then she seemed on the shorter side. Her heart-shaped face was the color of vanilla yogurt, and a sprinkle of freckles crossed the bridge of her small nose. Unlike Anna's limp locks, her shoulder-length brown hair looked thick and almost seemed to bounce in rhythm with her steps. The scooped neckline of her aqua-blue designer shirt was a little low, something Anna would never wear, revealing a crystal daisy pendant necklace. Her jeans, which were tucked into her boots, were intentionally distressed. They looked a lot like Anna's, which really were old and worn. Anna had paid three bucks for hers at a thrift shop, but she was pretty sure this girl had dropped at least a hundred dollars on hers.

The girl tossed her bag onto the table, staring intently at the food in front of her.

Anna was about to say something when she noticed that everyone in the cafeteria was staring at them.

Bouncy Girl sat down across from her and leaned in. "You should probably leave," she whispered, her eyes still focused on her lunch tray.

Anna's smile fell from her face as if she'd just been slapped. Her first reaction was to be defensive and tell

Bouncy Girl that if anyone was leaving, it wasn't going to be her. But Anna didn't like confrontation, and she especially didn't want to start something on her second day at a new school. As she reached for her tray, Bouncy Girl added, "People don't really talk to me. So if you want to make friends here, you won't want to sit anywhere near me."

"Oh. Well, uh, do you want me to move to another table?" Anna blurted out.

"Do what you want," Bouncy Girl said with a shrug. "But don't say I didn't warn you. Unpopularity is like a disease, and especially around me, it's definitely contagious."

Anna glanced around the room. If she got up now, where would she go? She decided to make the best of this. "On second thought, I'll take my chances," Anna said, not moving. She kind of wondered if the girl was throwing a pity party for herself and liked to be dramatic. But then again, the attention from the rest of the room was hard to miss.

"Do these people always stare like this?" Anna asked in a low voice.

"All the time."

"That's stupid. Why?" Anna couldn't help being curious.

"They don't like me," the girl muttered.

"Right. That's a good reason," Anna snorted. "By the way, I'm Anna."

"I know."

They sat and ate together in silence, but at least it wasn't the awkward kind that made Anna want to run screaming from the room. And she definitely preferred that over the gawking from the last table.

As she finished her apple, her messenger bag started vibrating against her feet, startling her. It was as if it had a mind of its own.

Pulling it out, she saw a new text.

Meet me after school at the cemetery—Millie

Millie? How did she get the number? Even Anna didn't know what the phone number was. And she had told Millie the battery was dead, so how did Millie know she'd get the message?

"So weird," Anna mumbled.

"That must've been important, huh?"

Anna looked up at Bouncy Girl; she'd forgotten she was there. "Not really. I was just surprised."

"Yeah, I'm surprised whenever I get a message too." Bouncy Girl looked down at her lap as she rotated her gold bracelet several times. Anna felt bad for her. Nobody deserved to be completely alone.

Suddenly Bouncy Girl looked straight at Anna. "I

have an idea." A smile slowly crept across her face. "Let's exchange numbers."

The hopeful look in her eyes tore at Anna's heart. She couldn't very well tell her it wasn't her phone; the girl had watched her get a text message on it only seconds earlier. And to tell her that, she'd have to tell the whole story, and she wasn't sure she wanted to do that either.

"Okay." Anna nodded. "Except . . . I'm not exactly sure what the number is for this phone. It's kinda new." She hoped that didn't sound too lame, but at least that was the truth.

"It's fine. Let me put my number in yours."

Anna handed her phone over and watched as the girl added her number and then used it to call her own phone. "All set. Now I have your number too." She held her phone up so Anna could see what the number to her new mystery phone really was, just before the bell rang.

"See ya around!" said Bouncy Girl as she seemed to bounce away, her mood definitely lifted.

Anna gave a small wave, but her smile was completely wiped from her face as she looked down and saw Bouncy Girl's name in her phone.

She was the girl Olivia had been making fun of the day before.

Lucy Edwards.

CHAPTER 9
ANNA

After school, Anna dropped off her books in her room, then quickly slipped out her back gate. She still thought it was kind of strange that Millie wanted to meet at the cemetery. But even stranger? She spotted Millie in the grass, sitting on a small, spread-out blanket, shaded by a large oak, with her backpack at her feet. She looked like she was ready for a picnic with the dead. Other than her, the place was deserted.

"Hey," Anna called out. Millie looked up as she walked over, and smiled as Anna sat down next to her. Her legs were wedged between the graves of Margaret Meyers, to Millie's right, and Dorothy Quinn on her left.

Anna hoped Millie hadn't seen her come out of the house. "So, what made you choose these friends?" Anna asked, nodding toward the graves.

"Actually," said Millie, "I felt kind of bad for this one." She moved to the side so Anna could see the gravestone behind her. It read JANE DOE. "Sad, right?" she sighed. "She doesn't have any flowers. Nobody even knows she's here."

Anna nodded. "Yeah, that is sad."

"I guess not many people visit this cemetery. Some think it's haunted. Especially at midnight. Or deadtime."

Anna raised an eyebrow.

"Deadtime," Millie explained, "is three a.m., when the spirits of the dead are most active. Or so I've heard."

"Yeah, well, I don't believe in all that ghost stuff."

"Me neither. So, I got something for you!" Millie said, changing the subject. She grabbed her schoolbag, pulled out a bunch of bundled cords, and set them in front of Anna.

"What's this?"

"It's for your phone."

"*My* phone?"

"You know, the one you found." She handed Anna a pink sparkly case. "I think this will fit it. And I had an extra charger, and headphones, and—"

"I can't take all this."

"Sure you can! It's just sitting around collecting dust. I don't need it anymore. And now we can actually text each other." Millie seemed more excited than Anna.

"Well . . . thanks." Maybe she could charge the phone and then look through it and figure out who it belonged to.

"No problem." Millie waved her hand dismissively. "So . . . you've practically taken over as the most talked-about girl in school."

Anna nodded. "It's like I can feel the whispers and eyes of the entire school every time I move."

"It probably didn't help that you just sat in Olivia's seat, at *her* lunch table," Millie laughed. "Trying to take her place already?"

"What?" Anna asked, horrified. No wonder that group had all looked at her in shock at first. Could she have made a worse decision? Only two days at the school and she'd stolen the most popular girl's seat at lunch.

Millie smiled ruefully, as if reading her mind. "It'll go away."

"You think?" Anna asked.

Millie shrugged. "I've seen the wrath of Olivia. And usually the damages don't last for too long. Once she finds something new in her path to destroy, you'll be old news."

"I hope you're right. She doesn't bother you, right?"

"I've been blending in forever. But whatever. I gave up on the popular thing a long time ago. I pretty much consider popularity evil."

Anna picked up a piece of grass and smoothed it with her nail. "So what wrath did you witness?"

Millie paused. "Olivia caught some girl kissing her boyfriend."

"Johnny?"

"What? No, Johnny's not her boyfriend. At least, I don't think so."

Anna felt her heart beat faster with this news.

"So who was the guy?" Anna asked.

Millie ducked her head. "I'm sure you wouldn't know him."

"Try me," Anna said.

Millie shrugged. "Some guy named Spencer."

"Spencer?" Anna echoed. She looked at Millie and noticed she was biting back a smile. Did Millie like that arrogant nerdy-cute guy with the camera?

"Have you met him?" Millie asked.

Anna nodded. "He just helped me with my locker this morning."

"Hmm," Millie said. As she rambled on about her classes, Anna's mind was still dwelling on Johnny's not having a girlfriend. Spencer was kind of cute in a nerdy sort of way, but he was totally off-limits if Millie liked him. And it really surprised her that Olivia liked him too. She seemed more like a girl who preferred football players.

Like Johnny.

"Can I ask you something?" Anna leaned in.

"Sure."

"I ran into this creepy guy around here yesterday morning. And"—she lowered her voice to a whisper— "he threatened me."

"Seriously? What did he look like?"

As Anna described the guy to her, Millie wrinkled her forehead. "I think I know who it was. His name's Vincent. He sounds psycho, but I wouldn't worry too much about him. His bark is worse than his bite."

Anna's eyes widened. "You know him?"

"Yeah. He's a senior and went to our school a few years back. He's homeschooled now. I heard he does odd jobs around town. I guess that includes cemetery groundskeeper."

"A psycho cemetery groundskeeper. Great."

"He sounds like a jerk. Probably was trying to scare you. Just ignore him. I doubt you'll run into him again. It's not like you're over here every day or something."

"What? No, of course not. Why would I be over here every day?" Anna giggled, biting her bottom lip.

"Okay, well, I gotta run." Millie stood up, dusting off the back of her pants. "Lots of homework."

"Me too." Anna helped Millie shove the blanket into her bag. "Thanks for all the stuff."

"No prob. Text me later?"

"Sure." Anna gathered up the phone equipment but waited until Millie had turned the corner and was out of sight before walking the few feet back to her house.

• • •

As soon as Anna got home, she charged the phone, then scrolled through the contacts. There wasn't much there. Just some random numbers without any names. The initials *AT* were next to one number. There were some photos stored in the picture folder: a Halloween mask, a headstone with a blurry name. Was it Ashley Martin? Ashton Marvin? Anna couldn't tell.

And then there were several text messages saved from AT. She read through the latest conversation:

I've got it.

Great. You remember what to do?

Of course. It's all set.

Remember—don't breathe a word of this.

Right.

No contacts, no photos of friends, only a few texts . . . it was like whoever owned the phone had known they were going to lose it. Or been afraid it might fall into the wrong hands.

Creepy.

CHAPTER 10

ANNA

The rest of the week flew by. It was finally Friday, which meant that all day, Anna overheard conversations about weekend plans. By the time school was over, it was clear that she would be doing the one thing everybody seemed to be talking about: going to the Ashbury party.

Back in Sacramento, Anna had spent her weekends doing homework and writing in her journal, or with her nose buried in a good book. Every weekend. And she wouldn't admit it to anyone, but she used to dream about being popular—having more friends than she could count and plans that always seemed to conflict with other plans she forgot she had already made.

Millie wasn't in class, so Anna headed to the lunch line alone. She grabbed an apple and a bottle of water and paid the cashier before heading toward the empty table by the fire exit. She expected to see the familiar faces of the two brothers who sometimes sat there quietly, playing on their phones.

But today was different. Only one person sat there. A girl. With blue eyes and bouncy hair.

Lucy.

Anna hadn't talked to her since Tuesday at lunch, when Lucy had given Anna her number. It wasn't like she had been avoiding her; Lucy just hadn't been around.

Through all the whispers and stares since, Anna still had no idea why Lucy was one of the least liked girls in the school, but she had an idea it must have something to do with Olivia. It seemed Olivia could make you or break you, when it came to school.

Anna felt awkward. Should she go sit with Lucy or walk outside and find a spot away from everyone?

Anna made a quick turn and walked to the cafeteria exit. Once she made it into the courtyard beside the cafeteria, she began to relax. A few students were eating lunch and reading. She decided she'd pick one of these benches and make the outdoors her new lunch spot. Well, when the weather allowed it.

Anna tossed her messenger bag onto the bench and made herself comfy while pulling out her journal. Pencil in hand and notebook in lap, she started writing as she nibbled on her apple. The sunlight beaming down on her quickly warmed her, despite the cool breeze.

Then a shadow fell over her and she looked up. Olivia stood there, smirking. Instead of saying anything, Anna sat there silently, staring back at her like an idiot. How did this girl have so much power over her?

"Annabel," Olivia said, tilting her head to the side. "Are you still coming to my party tonight?"

"Yeah. Sure." Although Anna didn't feel so sure. Was this Olivia's way of trying to uninvite her?

"Okay. Well, Eden thought you might need the address." Olivia handed her a folded-up piece of paper. "Unless you have a phone now?" She raised a questioning eyebrow.

Anna shook her head, taking the paper.

"Didn't think so. Well, see you tonight. And by the way, good decision you made in the lunchroom." Olivia winked, flipped her straight hair over her bony shoulder, and walked away.

• • •

The music blared as Anna made her way up the driveway to the Ashbury mansion. In her old neighborhood, people would have been shaking their fists and complaining about this kind of noise coming through their thin walls and into their closet-sized apartments. Here, the nearest neighbor was a quarter mile away.

Anna walked up to a massive stone entryway and rang the bell, and a maid answered the door, ushering her through the house to the backyard, where a covered pool area opened out onto the beach. Anna felt as if she had just walked onto a movie set. White chaise lounges flanked the pool, and hundreds of tea lights decorated the area.

The deck was crowded with people, talking and dancing to the blaring music. She could feel the bass vibrating through the floor. There was a snack table on one side of the deck and a DJ on the other. It was the loudest, most chaotic scene Anna had ever witnessed.

She spotted Johnny and Olivia and headed toward them. At the same moment another girl who apparently also had her eyes on Johnny bounded toward them.

"Johnny!" the girl screamed.

"Hi, Olivia." Anna gave a slight wave.

"Hey, Anna." Olivia smiled coolly. "Glad you made it."

Anna let out a nervous laugh. "Thanks for inviting me. Your home is so . . ."

"Magnificent? Surreal? Fit for a queen?" Olivia suggested.

"Uh, yes. Definitely. All of the above," Anna said, not sure whether Olivia was joking.

Olivia's ice-white hair was pinned up in a twist, with long tendrils hanging down. Her lips were stained pink and her eyelids were made up with a smoky eye shadow. And of course she was wearing pink from head to toe. Her skirt had a slit up the side, and her satiny shirt was almost backless, with a plunging neckline in the front. Anna knew her mom would kill her if she even *thought* about wearing an outfit like that.

"That's Harper," Olivia said, looking at the girl talking to Johnny.

"Did I hear my name?" The girl draped an arm across Olivia's shoulder.

"This is Annabel. She's new." Olivia unenthusiastically waved her hand in Anna's direction as if she were swishing away a pesky fly.

"Right. The new girl. Hi," Harper said sweetly.

Johnny took a sip from his cup. "So where's your sister, Olivia?"

Olivia frowned. "How should I know? We're not joined at the hip." She turned to Anna. "It's funny. People think twins have this whole mind-connection thing, but we don't."

"You sure?" Eden appeared next to them, smiling, almost as if the timing had been planned.

"I knew it!" shouted Johnny.

Everyone laughed except Olivia. Eden stood close to Johnny, tilting her head toward him, her diamond earrings catching the light.

The closest Anna had ever come to owning diamonds was a pair of cubic zirconia stud earrings given to her by her grandma. They were so shiny and dazzling, she'd thought for sure they were the real thing. Until a week later, when they'd turned her ears green.

"You know," Eden said, studying Anna, "with some new clothes and a little makeup, you'd look awesome. Fit right in."

"Um, thanks?" Anna looked over at Johnny and Harper staring at her curiously. What was she supposed to say?

"Great. I have a fabulous hairdresser I can recommend."

"My mom does my hair."

"Your mom?" Olivia snickered. "That explains a lot."

"Don't listen to her." Eden waved her hand at her sister. "I can take you to my girl. She's fabulous!"

"I meant, my mom is a hairdresser. Actually, she works at Twisted." Anna nervously rotated her silver bracelets around her wrist. Could she possibly stumble over her words more if she tried?

"Who's your mom?" Eden asked.

"Valerie Craven. She—"

Eden raised an eyebrow. "Val is your mom?"

Anna nodded.

"No way! That's who we go to! Olivia, check it out, Val is Anna's mom."

Anna could feel her face getting red. In what universe was her mom more popular than she was?

"Whatever." Olivia looked down at her phone. "Hey, Harper, do me a fave and check the ice, pretty please?" Olivia smiled sweetly and batted her long lashes. "If it's running low, just tell the help, okay? Thanks."

Harper walked away without saying a word. Anna wondered if she was actually going to let Olivia order her around like that.

"She seems nice," Anna found herself saying lamely, just to break the silence.

Eden turned to her and whispered in her ear, "You should be careful. Not everyone is who they pretend to be."

Johnny checked his phone, frowning.

"What's wrong?" Eden asked.

"Nothin'. Just a text."

Olivia peered over Johnny's shoulder as he held the screen out to show her.

"Oh geez, give me that!" Olivia swiped Johnny's phone right out of his hand. Laughing, she pushed a few buttons, then handed it back to him.

"Done. Problem solved," she said with a smirk.

Eden laughed. "She probably butt-dialed you. I wouldn't be surprised if she had you on *all* her speed dials."

Anna had no idea who *she* could be. But whoever it was, they obviously didn't like her.

Anna stood self-consciously as Eden and Olivia pulled Johnny off into the crowd. She loved people-watching, but she felt kind of alone. Everyone seemed to be hanging within their own cliques. Anna knew she should be bold. She'd have to meet new people some-time. So she walked over to a group of guys and girls. A guy with sandy-brown hair who looked like a skater and was holding some girl's hand was talking about riding the waves. Anna stood nearby and listened to the end of a story he was telling.

"That's awesome, Mike," a guy said. "You're so lucky he didn't catch you."

The group shifted slightly and Anna was suddenly boxed out. Feeling awkward, she turned to walk away, knowing she wasn't blending, and bumped into a girl with dark brown hair and expensive highlights, spilling her drink all over her.

"Watch it!" the girl shouted.

"I'm so sorry!" Anna was mortified. She looked around for napkins, but the girl stormed off.

Anna wandered over to a snack table. Maybe coming here had been a mistake. Another girl was crunching away on some chips, scanning the crowd.

"Millie!" Anna exclaimed, relief washing over her. "I wasn't expecting to see you." She felt guilty about not telling her about the party, but Millie hadn't said anything to her either about coming. *I guess we're even,* she thought, grabbing a handful of pretzels.

"Yeah, well, I'm not supposed to be here." Millie smiled mischievously.

Anna frowned. "What do you mean?"

Millie shrugged. "I wasn't invited."

"You snuck in?"

"Sure. Nobody tells me who I can or can't hang around with. Especially the Ashbury twins."

Anna had to give her props for being brave. If it were her, she'd be looking over her shoulder every second, afraid of getting caught and tossed out.

"So, I just saw you spill soda all over that girl." Millie laughed.

Anna winced. "I didn't mean to."

"Oh, I don't care. It's funny. She's one of the Ashburys' little projects. She probably deserves it."

"Projects?" Anna repeated.

"Yeah, they gave her a makeover and she suddenly went from a nobody to a somebody. Like, who does that?"

Anna nodded, although she could kind of understand it. Who didn't want to be a somebody?

"So when did you get your invitation? That day you went to the Corner Café?" Millie asked.

"Well, yeah. But . . . ," Anna began.

Millie's eyebrows shot up. "I don't care. Besides, who'd turn down an Ashbury invitation anyways?"

"You mean besides you?"

"I'm here, aren't I?" Millie laughed. "So you like Johnny, huh?"

Anna felt herself blush uncontrollably. "No, of course not."

"Okay. Sure," Millie said knowingly.

Anna felt her cheeks turn even pinker. "Okay. Fine. Maybe a little. Not that I stand a chance."

"You never know," Millie said, nudging her.

"Well, I'm not after him or anything. Besides, there must be a ton of cute guys from school." *Who Olivia doesn't like,* she silently added.

"Most of them are rich jerks," Millie said softly. "And the girls are all two-faced."

"That's harsh. Some of the people must be okay," Anna said hopefully.

Millie's eyes darkened. "I wish it wasn't, but it's totally true. Take my advice and steer clear of them. Especially the Ashbury twins."

Anna looked at Millie with confusion. "So why even come to this party, then?"

Millie smiled. "To have a little fun."

Anna smiled back. "Oh yeah?"

Millie winked, then disappeared into the sea of unfamiliar faces. Anna was alone again. Trying to figure out where she should go, she spun around and heard a crash.

Her purse had just knocked over a crystal vase of white roses on the table next to her.

"Are you okay?" Eden asked, walking over.

"I'm so sorry!" Anna said, automatically dropping her purse and stooping down to help clean up the broken vase and flowers.

"Oh, don't worry about it," Eden said as a couple of servers hurried over and began sweeping up the mess.

The white roses were in a pool of water on the floor around Anna's feet. She couldn't believe she had been so clumsy. She had the worst luck ever.

"Be careful!" A heavyset woman walked toward them with towels and a bag for the broken glass and flowers.

Just as the woman issued her warning, Anna felt a piece of glass slice into her finger. Drops of blood escaped and stained one of the white roses on the floor. Anna had an uneasy, sinking feeling in the pit of her stomach.

She should have paid attention.

CHAPTER 11

Lucy

That very same night, a party of one was happening at the residence of Lucy Edwards. Playing the part of a stressed fashionista with an undecided mind and an uncanny tendency toward the lateness she usually so despised, Lucy focused on her wardrobe while taking deep breaths. And counting.

One, two . . . She flung a white button-up silk blouse over her desk chair. It made her complexion look ghostly and washed-out.

Three . . . And kicked off the cute tan kitten heels with peekaboo toes. They squished her feet like a medieval torture device.

Four, five, six . . . She slam-dunked a black skirt into her wastebasket. Black was too goth for a graveyard date.

Seven, eight . . . Ooh, that bloodred V-neck really emphasized her long, graceful neck. And . . .

Nine . . . Where was she? She'd lost track.

Lucy let out a dramatic sigh and crumpled onto her bed. She would never find anything to wear.

She chanted quietly under her breath. *I will not panic. I will not panic.*

Although the more she said it, the quicker she chanted, until it sounded like, *I will panic, I will panic.*

What was she so worried about, anyway? It wasn't like she'd never met up with John before. Except this time she was meeting him at the graveyard. At night. By herself. Okay, so maybe it sounded like the beginning of a really bad slasher film, but Lucy had to remind herself she would be seeing the love of her life tonight. And it would probably be super romantic. She could just picture it.

She'd be standing underneath a dark sky, which would be glittering with millions of stars that twinkled almost, but not quite, brighter than John's eyes. John would see her and time would stand still. Her hair would be perfect. His smile would be perfect.

Everything would be perfect.

Lucy closed her eyes, imagining how it would feel to have John's arms around her. . . .

SMACK!

The background music in her head came to a screeching halt.

"Oww! What the heck?" Lucy vigorously rubbed the side of her face, trying to ease the pain inflicted by her bedroom wall. If this had been one of those cheesy cartoons, she would be seeing stars orbiting around her right now. Or was it birds?

Whatever. Lucy shook her head. Things would not end with her and John running into each other.

Unless, of course, it was her lips running into his face.

Lucy decided to simply give up trying to make decisions. She walked over to her closet and picked the first top she saw. The same with her skirt. And the winning purse and shoes were the ones closest to her.

The outcome? She looked fabulous.

Lucy grabbed her phone to text him, not caring that he'd told her not to. She would make it short.

On my way.

She buttoned up her long black coat and dashed out the front door.

Walking clumsily through loose gravel in her heels, Lucy focused on her phone as a new text message popped up on her screen. It was from John.

That's okay. See you soon.

Lucy was completely submerged in the message, smiling as she reread it several times, unaware of the headlights rushing straight toward her.

HOOOONNNNK!

She jumped to the side as the car swerved wide, barley missing her. She twisted her right ankle as she landed, catching herself on the nearest tree, scraping her hand on the rough bark.

"Stupid driver!" she yelled back over her shoulder, although the car was already long gone.

She rubbed her ankle, hoping it wasn't sprained. As far as she could tell, it wasn't swollen. She would just have to walk more carefully. What had she been thinking, choosing heels as tall as stilts to walk through gravel and dirt?

Checking the time on her phone, she saw she was only a few minutes late. She was about a minute from the cemetery—she was making better time than she thought. From the side entrance, all looked still. No shadowy figures lurking around the headstones. No hot guys named John sitting on any of the benches waiting impatiently for their beautiful girlfriend.

Hmm . . . she hoped he'd gotten her text and didn't think she'd stood him up. "John?" Lucy said in a loud whisper as she walked carefully down the path through the center of the cemetery. Where did he say to meet him? By the mausoleums? That must be those huge buildings to the right. She took a shortcut through the grass, careful to not fall and twist her other ankle and carefully avoiding stepping directly on the grave markers.

Lucy heard a twig snap to her left. She stopped walking and listened.

"John? Is that you?"

No response.

She took another step just as she saw movement out of the corner of her eye. There was no mistaking it this time. But before she could see who or what it was, several things happened.

A loud noise. Screaming.

A bright light blinded her.

More screaming—possibly her own.

Falling. It seemed to last forever.

And then complete darkness.

CHAPTER 12

ANNA

Anna couldn't leave the party fast enough. She called her mom for a ride, but it went straight to voice mail. She left a message for her, but she was probably asleep already after working all day.

Anna took the shortest route home—through the graveyard, careful to stay on the lit path.

Something in the grass caught her eye. Anna slowly reached into her front pocket for the phone. The glow from the screen was so bright she didn't need the flashlight. She waved the phone over the grass. A shiny object reflected off the light, sparkling like a diamond.

It *was* a diamond. She picked it up. A diamond earring. And it looked like a match to the pair Eden was wearing. She had definitely committed those to memory. But how did Eden lose that out here, in the cemetery?

The only explanation was that someone else had a similar pair. Anna stuffed the earring in her front pocket.

The phone vibrated in her palm. A new text.

Can you help me?

Anna shook her head in disbelief before responding.

Not my phone. Sorry.

She had barely sent the text before a new one appeared.

You're my only hope. You're the only one who can help.

Help with what? Anna's curiosity took over. Whoever this phone belonged to definitely had friends with lots of issues.

**My grave needs flowers. I'm the only one
without flowers. Nobody remembers me.**

Anna nearly dropped the phone. She looked behind her, her eyes darting from one grave to the next. She picked up her pace until she was nearly running. It didn't make any sense. None of this did.

Who are you? Anna typed.

She pulled open the gate to her backyard, then quickly shut it behind her. As if the wrought-iron barrier could protect her from whatever was pranking her.

**Jane Doe. And I'm wedged in between
Margaret Meyers and Dorothy Quinn, two
horrible old snoots I can't get away from.**

Stop playing, Anna texted back.

Could Millie be any more obvious? And if she thought this was funny, she was crazy. Anna was totally regretting that Millie had her number.

She frowned. Why would Millie do this? Anna hadn't said goodbye when she'd left the party. Maybe she was mad about that?

Anna froze before reaching the porch steps of the Manor. All the windows were dark. She didn't really feel like being alone right now, especially since it was still before her curfew.

Instead of asking herself questions about Millie she didn't have the answers to, she should confront her. She texted her:

> Just stop sending me weird texts and meet me at the park by the swings.

Winchester Park was just around the corner from her house, but walking there seemed to take forever. She swallowed several times, her mouth dry, as she quickened her pace and ignored the urge to run back home every time she saw a shadow or heard an owl. She kept looking over her shoulder, half expecting to see someone.

Like maybe a creepy graveyard groundskeeper.

Keeping her head down, she focused on taking calm, even breaths. Her steps slowed as the concrete sidewalk turned into pavement and she approached the playground.

The silver slide to her right was dented and scuffed. Anna jumped as she heard a creak that quickly turned into a series of shrieking sounds near the swing sets.

Her knuckles turned white as she clenched her phone, shining its light in that direction.

There were two sagging swings.

One of them began to stir.

It swung back and forth, slowly at first, as though being pumped by invisible legs. Because right now there wasn't any wind. Not even a slight breeze.

Childlike giggles floated through the air.

The chains groaned with an invisible weight as the swing went faster. Higher.

Anna bit her bottom lip. She spun herself in a circle, with the small beam from the phone shaking in her hands.

No one was there. She was alone.

Anna backed away with quick, jerky steps, gasping as the back of her legs hit something.

"Oh! It's just a bench." She held a hand over her chest as if trying to keep her heart from jumping out, then sat down. The wooden boards dug into her back. Her gaze slid back to the swings, both completely still.

It was just her imagination again. The swing had never been moving—that was just silly.

Movement out of the corner of her eye caused her to look over at the monkey bars. In the distance, someone was waving their arms in her direction. The moonlight didn't offer enough light to see who it was, but it had to be Millie. They would probably talk about her not-so-funny and slightly annoying sense of humor when it came to those text messages and then laugh as Anna told her about her crazy imagination and what a chicken she had been.

Anna stood up and walked along the paved pathway that separated the park from the street. But then she realized Millie wasn't there anymore.

Nobody was.

Dead leaves clung to the bottom of her shoes, and the pungent whiff of skunk floated past her as she covered her nose with the sleeve of her sweater.

"Don't freak out," she whispered to herself.

She faced her fear head-on, proving to herself that she'd imagined it all as she walked back and sat motionless on one of the swings, her hands gripping the cold metal chains. She kept checking the phone, thinking Millie would at least text back to let her know if she would be there soon. Or not at all.

She'd give her a few more minutes and then she was out of there. But only because she was tired. And cold.

Anna felt a hand against her back, gently pushing her forward.

"Finally! You totally scared me—" The words died on Anna's lips as she looked behind her.

Nobody was there.

"Hi."

Anna spun her head forward and stared into a pair of gray eyes that didn't belong to Millie.

Anna jumped off the swing, stumbling, staring at a little boy who looked about five years old. The corners of his lips pulled up into a gap-toothed grin. His mouth was rimmed with dirt and sand clung to his curls. As he sleepily rubbed a fist against one eye, he giggled. The same sound Anna had heard earlier.

"Are you lost?" Anna's voice shook. She didn't see anyone else nearby, and something about this whole situation screamed weirdness.

The little boy shook his head, yawning. He pulled a handful of rocks from his jeans pocket, holding his palm out to display his treasure to Anna.

"Have you seen my gold rock?" He looked up at Anna with huge, innocent eyes.

"Um, no. No, sorry." Anna shook her head. "Did you lose it around here?"

"I can't find it. It's my favoritest."

"What's your name?"

"Tommy. I'm four," he said proudly, holding up five fingers.

"Okay, Tommy, how about we walk you back to your house. Where do you live?" Anna squatted down to his level.

"There!" He pointed toward the ground by Anna's feet.

She looked down, catching a glimpse of gold. "Is this your rock?" Anna picked it up and wiped it on her jeans, dusting off the sand.

"Yes!" The little boy excitedly plucked it from her hand.

"Can you—" Anna stopped midsentence as the boy waved his right hand.

"Bye," he said in a small voice.

"Where are you going?" Anna blinked, watching the figure of the little boy slowly fade in and out while standing in front of her, until suddenly he was gone. Just like that. Vanished into thin air right in front of her eyes.

Anna didn't—couldn't—take her eyes from the spot. She stayed frozen in place, reaching her hand out in front of her where the boy had stood only seconds ago, a hallucination. Standing up, she slowly walked backward, her eyes never leaving that spot, as if she expected the hallucination to return any minute.

When it didn't, she took off at a run, catching the sweet smell of chocolate and the distant laughter of a little boy.

CHAPTER 13

Lucy

Weak morning light touched Lucy's face as she sat up. Birds sang in the branches above her. The air was cool. She shook some leaves off her skirt, trying to wrap her mind around why she was in . . . the graveyard?

Had she been outside all night? Did someone dump her there?

Lucy stood up, her legs shaky. She felt a little off. She seemed to glide in her muddy heels, rather than step. She was graceful, not clumsy and awkward. And she felt a bit light-headed.

Walking up to the narrow winding road that led to her house, she inspected her body for bruises, scrapes, cuts, or gashes. None. Weirdly, she felt like she'd had a full night's rest.

I slept in a cemetery. With dead people. Lucy shuddered.

She ran her fingers through her tangled hair, trying to rake out imagined bugs. She didn't remember much, just walking outside and then waking up just now. It was like she'd passed out or fainted. Out like a light.

A light . . .

That triggered something, a memory right on the edge of discovery.

She had been looking for John and then . . . then she'd walked right into a bright, shining light. But what was that light? Her memories seemed to end there.

Lucy looked up, realizing she was already at her front door. She didn't live far from the cemetery, but it should've taken her at least fifteen minutes to walk home. Not two.

Lucy tried to turn the knob but her hand went through it. *Through* it! Lucy squeezed her eyes shut, then placed her hand in front of her nose, inspecting it. Solid as any hand should be.

Looking down, she noticed something very strange. Her feet weren't actually touching the ground. They hovered an inch above it.

Swallowing, she reached for the doorknob again, slowly, watching in amazement as her hand went through it once more.

"Freaky."

She pushed her whole hand against the door, and it slipped in just as easily, so she continued to push her entire body right through to the other side, where she floated above the hardwood floors in her foyer.

The house was quiet. Lucy was disappointed her parents were still at work. She wasn't sure what was happening, and she didn't feel like figuring it out on her own. She pulled out her phone, grasping it without a problem.

She needed help.

CHAPTER 14

ANNA

The buzzing of the phone woke Anna, destroying any chance of sleeping in. And she definitely needed it, since she had obviously been sleep deprived and her imagination was overactive lately.

Anna yawned, wishing she could just stay in bed all weekend. If she didn't start unpacking some of her things, though, her mom would throw a fit. She looked at the most recent message on the phone.

Quit playing games. I need to talk to you.

Anna shook her head. Clearly she was missing half of this one-sided conversation.

If you don't know who this phone belongs to, then maybe you have the wrong number? Anna texted back.

No response. Nice. They must've gotten the hint. Unfortunately, that still left her not knowing who the phone belonged to.

The phone vibrated in her hand with a new message.

> **Can you help me?**

This had to be someone different. Maybe now she could get to the bottom of this.

> **Who are you trying to reach?**
>
> **You!**
>
> **Look, I just found this phone. It's not even mine.**
>
> **But I need YOUR help. You're my only hope.**
>
> **Who is this?**
>
> **Lucy.**

Lucy? Anna rubbed her eyes, checking the name at the top of the screen: *Lucy Edwards*. Anna debated responding. She didn't want to encourage her, but she didn't want to be rude either.

> **Hi, Lucy. What's up?**

> Who's this?

Huh? Anna shook her head. Maybe Lucy had several messages going at once and couldn't keep track. She texted Lucy back.

> This is Anna.
>
> Anna from school?
>
> Yep.

How many other Annas did she know?

> I don't know what's going on. My parents are fighting and ...
>
> And?
>
> And they said some really weird things.
>
> Maybe you should talk to them, then.

Anna had no idea why Lucy needed her help for something like that.

> I tried. They don't hear me.

Anna frowned.

Talk louder?

Not funny. I'm dead serious. Need to get air . . .
just meet me at the cemetery. Please. Need
your help.

Anna's mind flashed back to last night. No way was she meeting Lucy there. She considered, for like two seconds, that maybe Lucy really needed help. But . . . someone else could help her, right? It didn't need to be her. And meeting her at the cemetery wouldn't really help her situation, so she shouldn't feel guilty.

Sorry, I have no way to get there. But I'll see
you Monday and we can talk at lunch!

It's okay. I'll just come to you.

A shiver ran down Anna's spine. Lucy didn't know where she lived . . . did she? She pushed the power button on the phone and nothing happened. She flipped it over and, with her nail, pried the back off, taking out the square, flat battery. The screen went dark.

Anna let out a huge sigh of relief.

She was beginning to understand why people at school thought Lucy was strange. Oh well, not her problem.

She pulled the covers back up to her chin, wishing she could just ignore the rest of the world.

A loud thump echoed from downstairs.

Anna leaped out of bed, taking her tangled comforter with her, and stumbled several times before making it across her room. She yanked open her bedroom door and peered into the dark hallway.

"Mom?" Anna called. Her mom was at work, but maybe she'd forgotten something and come back home to get it.

No answer.

She slid on her fuzzy slippers and made her way down the stairs two at a time.

The living room was empty. Everything seemed normal. Well, almost. A chunky vintage clock lay on the ground. That thing was definitely heavy enough to cause a noise loud enough to hear up in her room.

Grunting, she moved the un-ticking, brassy object out of the way and propped it against the wall. The nail above was at an angle, obviously bent from the weight. Even at their old apartment, stuff was always falling, dropping, or doing something strange, and she was never freaked out *this* much.

But now it looked as if their bad luck had followed them here.

Anna grabbed a breakfast bar from the kitchen and

headed back upstairs to unpack, cranking up her music to earsplitting levels—a guaranteed way to drown out the noise of any other objects that might happen to randomly thump, bang, smack, or cause any sound that would make her heart miss a beat.

Or any random, uninvited person who might happen to ring the doorbell.

CHAPTER 15

ANNA

Monday morning, on the way to her locker, Anna walked past two girls whispering, catching only some of their words.

"Girl . . . crashed . . . Ashbury . . . party."

"Yeah . . . it is," her friend whispered back.

Anna was suddenly embarrassed. Why would they think she crashed the party? The twins had invited her. Actually, Eden had. But that was the same thing, right?

Or maybe they meant how she crashed *at* the party. The girl with the soda. The vase.

She tried not to look around at the people who were gossiping about her. It was hard to ignore them, but she did her best.

As she reached inside her locker for her books, she froze in horror. A dried-out white rose hung upside down from the top of her locker. Drops of red stained the petals on the left side.

Anna quickly turned, looking behind her. Nobody seemed to be watching. But . . . who had put that rose there? And what did it mean? Was it one of the roses from the party?

It had to be. Whoever put it there had definitely been at the party.

Anna needed to talk to Millie. She seemed to know everyone at school. Maybe she would have an idea who had done this.

Maybe Creepy Crypt Keeper had a brother.

Anna swallowed. How had someone gotten into her locker? The only people who knew the combination were herself, the school secretary, and . . . Spencer! He had helped her that one morning. Had he come back and put the rose in her locker? She didn't want to believe that, yet . . .

Maybe it was a prank. Someone could have gotten her combination from the principal's office. She racked her brain, trying to think who assisted Mrs. Clover during free period. Maybe her locker combo had even fallen out of her bag.

It was just some stupid joke to play on the new girl.

Lucky her.

Millie wasn't in first period. Or at lunch.

Anna pulled out the cell. She'd put the old battery back in, and luckily, it powered up, although it barely had any reception and the glow from the screen was dull. She texted her.

Hope you're not too sick. Miss you at school.

Anna set her phone on the table as she tried to eat the rest of her sandwich. She was taking a third bite when the phone beeped.

Millie's not here.

Anna texted back.

Who is this?

She didn't put the phone back down this time. She waited.

A text popped up.

Who is THIS?

Anna's fingers flew over the keys on her phone:

This is Anna. Millie's friend. Where is she?

Maybe Millie had a little brother or sister who was holding her phone.

Anna wondered if she should call Millie's phone.

A text came a moment later:

I found this phone Friday.

Where was Millie, and how had she lost her cell phone? Anna didn't bother texting back. She scrolled through her contacts and called Millie's phone.

A guy answered on the third ring. "Hello?"

"Hey. I just texted you about the phone you're using. It's my friend's phone and I'm trying to find her. Where did you find her phone?" Anna asked.

"I found it when I was leaving a party Friday night." His voice sounded familiar. "It was on the ground. I put it in my jacket pocket and forgot about it until it just started buzzing now when you texted."

That was when it hit her. If Millie had lost her phone Friday night before Anna left the party, then there's no way she could've been the one who pranked her. Maybe it was this guy? But that didn't explain how he would know about those exact names at the cemetery from that day.

"Who is this?" Anna asked suspiciously.

"Spencer."

"Spencer, it's Anna. Can you meet me so I can get Millie's phone back to her?"

"Okay," Spencer said. "I'll meet you by your locker after school. Hey, Anna?"

"Yeah?" she said.

"Who's Millie?"

. . .

After school Anna met up with Spencer and he handed over Millie's phone. Anna was surprised he didn't know Millie. "You know, short red hair, huge green eyes?" she prompted.

"Doesn't ring a bell." Spencer wiped a smudge off the lens of his camera.

Anna shrugged. Boys. She was meeting the girls at the Corner Café and was already running late. "Well, thanks for the phone." Anna would have to take it to Millie after the café.

"Sure. See ya." He paused, glancing up, and offered a quick smile before turning his full attention back to his camera.

At the Corner Café, Olivia and Eden were already at a table, complaining about a teacher they both had and the horrible amount of homework he gave out.

Great, more homework for me, Anna thought as she sat down. Eden looked up and smiled but continued complaining to her sister. Not that Anna really cared. Her thoughts were still on the rose she'd found in her locker, which she had stuffed into her messenger bag.

She rifled through her bag, the crisp leaves of the rose crinkling with the movement, then grabbed her textbook and plopped it on the table.

Olivia paused midsentence, turning to Anna. "Look at our little overachiever, eager to start her homework."

At least I do my own homework, Anna thought, wishing she had the courage to say it to Olivia's face. Instead, she just shrugged. A little piece of paper was sticking out of her book. She pulled it out. She hadn't lost her locker combo after all. She actually felt a little better as she swiped the paper from the book.

It wasn't her locker combo.

It was a photo. It looked like a page ripped out of the yearbook. But she had no idea how it had gotten there. Or why it was tucked between the pages of her book.

"What's that, Annabel?" Olivia interrupted her thoughts.

Anna looked over at her. "What?"

"That picture. Where did you get it?"

"Um, I just kind of found it."

"OMG!" Eden grabbed the photo from Anna. "Is this Lucy?"

Olivia looked over her shoulder. The silence at the table seemed to last an eternity.

"So sad." Eden frowned, her eyes glued to the photo. "Just so, so sad. It's like everything is a constant reminder of her today."

"Why is that sad?" Anna felt like she was missing part of the conversation.

"You know." Eden flipped through her notebook, glancing up at Anna. "The *accident*," she whispered.

"Accident?" Anna was beginning to feel like a parrot.

Olivia rolled her eyes. "Seriously? How can you *not* know about it? It's all over school." She slid a binder over to Anna. "I need this organized by date and subject."

"What happened?" Anna asked Eden.

"She had an accident in the cemetery," Eden told her. "Apparently she tripped and fell, hitting her head on a tombstone."

"Doesn't surprise me," said Olivia. "That girl was always a klutz."

"Geez, Liv, show some sensitivity." Eden glared at her twin before turning back to Anna. "It's really sad. Tragic, even."

"Yeah, well, she was so annoying," Olivia said, looking up as Johnny pulled up a chair at their table, setting his football helmet on the ground by his feet. He nodded to the group as he grabbed a book from his backpack and sat down.

"At least they're giving us time off to go to her funeral," Eden said.

Anna practically shot soda through her nose. "Funeral? You mean she *died*?"

"What do you think 'accident' means, gifted girl?" Olivia said, snorting.

"An accident could mean just an injury, genius," Anna snapped back, instantly wishing she could suck the words back in. The last thing she needed was to get on Olivia's bad side.

"I can't believe something like that happened . . . while we were at the party so close by," Johnny said. He started shredding pieces of his napkin.

Anna realized that those girls in the hall hadn't been whispering about her like she'd thought. They'd been whispering about Lucy.

"Yep. It must have been fate," Olivia said, raising her shoulders in a small, helpless shrug. "And here are our notes from third period for the last month. We need these typed, double-spaced." She plopped a small pile of papers held together with a binder clip in front of Anna.

Anna felt the heat rush to her face as Johnny watched the assignments pile up in front of her.

Johnny sighed, resting his elbows on the table. "I mean, what if I had just texted her on Friday? Maybe she wouldn't have gone out there and none of that would've happened."

"Friday night?" Anna stared at him. If the accident had been Friday . . . well, that was impossible. Lucy had texted her on Saturday. Maybe she died after she texted her on Saturday? But that didn't really make sense either.

"Yeah, it's all right here." Eden pushed her phone across the table to Anna.

The words on the lit-up screen seemed to jump out at Anna. "Her obituary," she whispered. With one finger, she scrolled through the text.

Lucille Edwards passed away Friday, October 17. She was found at Winchester Cemetery with a head injury. She will be sadly missed by her loving family. Lucy will be remembered for her sense of humor, creativity, and awkward hugs. A beloved daughter, she also leaves behind her older sister, Bea, and her best friend and bunny, Bun Bun.

Anna couldn't read on. She flicked the screen with her fingers, scrolling past the rest of the text. The screen rolled to a stop on a new obituary. The photo smiling back at Anna made her gasp.

"Are you okay?" Eden leaned in, catching a glimpse of the photo of a little boy.

Anna nodded, not trusting her voice. The familiar blond curls. The toothy smile. All that was missing was chocolate ice cream smeared around his mouth. And the name . . . it said his name was Thomas Jacobson. *Tommy.*

"No." Anna shook her head and slid the phone back to Eden.

"Oh, that's so sad!" Eden sounded choked up as she read her phone. "He was super young. Aw, and he loved collecting rocks! How cute is he?"

Anna felt light-headed.

"You act like you knew the kid or something," Olivia murmured. "You should be happier that we at least get a short school week." She took a sip of soda, pointing a finger at Anna. "And be on time in the morning, 'kay? I hate it when people make me wait on them."

Anna nodded, but inside she was rolling her eyes.

Nobody was really in the mood to study. And Anna was really not in the mood to have Olivia continue to bark orders at her. The group collected their books and began to head to the exit. Anna and Johnny were the last two at the table.

"Did you know her well?" Anna asked, breaking the silence. He seemed to be taking it the hardest.

Johnny shoved his books into his backpack.

She cleared her throat. "I mean, were you good friends or anything?"

Johnny suddenly looked up. "I don't want to talk about it." He scooped up his backpack and took off without saying another word. It was as if he couldn't leave quickly enough.

CHAPTER 16

ANNA

"How was work?" Anna asked.

Her mom paused between bites. "Good." She hadn't felt like cooking tonight, so they were just having turkey sandwiches and coleslaw from the deli. Anna didn't mind. She wasn't that hungry anyway. "I'm sorry to hear about that girl from your school," her mom said, sighing.

"I didn't really know her. But it's so sad."

Anna was afraid she might blurt something out about all the strange things happening around her lately. And *to* her. She didn't want to worry her mom and make her think she wasn't trying to adjust to their new life. Or worse, that she was going crazy like her great-uncle Maxwell.

Her mom wiped her hands on her jeans. "I want to talk to you."

"Sure. Everything okay?" Anna asked.

"I'm going to be gone this week. Just for a few days, though."

Anna put down her sandwich. "What? Where are you going?"

"I was offered a gig—makeup and hair for an Auto-rama show in Reno." Her face lit up. "This will be a great opportunity for me. It will help to bring in more money. And my friend Winston is close by, so if you need anything, he can help you."

"Winston?" That was the first time Anna had ever heard that name.

Her mom waved her hand dismissively. "Oh, he's just the mortician over at the mortuary here. He took over after Mr. Leavitt retired. But he's practically in our backyard, he's so close. So keep that in mind."

"Oh . . ." Anna nodded slowly, absorbing all this new information. The thought of being alone in the creepy mansion gave her chills. Normally she was perfectly fine being left alone, although it rarely happened. But lately things had been rubbing her the wrong way. The guy outside the house, the weird dreams, the spooky phone and texts. The hallucinations. Maybe it was nothing and she was overreacting, but she had also felt eyes on her more than once. And now her mom was going away, and if she needed anything, she'd have to ask the local undertaker? Someone who worked with the dead on a daily basis?

Not likely.

"I want you to feel okay with this," her mom said. "It's just such a great opportunity, and I didn't want to turn them down. . . ."

Anna shook her head. "No, Mom, it's fine. Really. You don't get many chances like this. I think you'll have fun."

Her mom grinned. "I'll call you every day." She gave Anna's shoulder a little squeeze and put her plate in the sink before padding down the hallway toward the stairs.

The phone buzzed in Anna's pocket. Thankfully, her mom had already left the room and was out of earshot.

Anna shoved a potato chip in her mouth as she walked to the library, reading the messages on the phone. She slammed the door behind her and turned the light on. Dust swirled around, dancing in the beam of light from the lamp. She flopped into an old leather chair, propping her feet up on the gigantic antique desk that sat in the middle of the room.

The library reminded Anna of a big dusty book.

Every time she walked in, she was overwhelmed by the aroma of leather and of cigar smoke from years past. The dark wooden decor and boat decorations were a dead giveaway that this room had belonged to Maxwell Maddsen. The floor-to-ceiling shelves that lined the room were filled with antique books, broken bindings as far as the eye could see. For some reason, Anna felt more at home in this room than any other place in the mansion.

She ran a finger over some of the leather spines. She needed to get lost in a good story . . . and forget about the horrible one she was living.

CHAPTER 17

ANNA

Millie was back at school the next day and was totally relieved to know Anna had her phone. She had no idea where she had lost it. Anna had decided not to mention how she'd tried to find Millie's house and bring it to her, since, when she mentioned the whole thing to her mom, her mom suggested that Millie might feel self-conscious about where she lived. Anna could appreciate that.

By the time she got home after school, storm clouds had rolled in and

the house was already dark. She shivered before making her way down the hallway to her room, turning on the lights as she went. Every creak seemed overly loud. She made sure not to look at her mom's empty room as she passed, not wanting to remind herself she was away. Anna felt strange being the only living thing in the house.

She changed her clothes and went back downstairs. She felt kind of uneasy . . . Could her stomach even handle food? The phone buzzed in her pocket, startling her out of her thoughts.

Have you decided to help me? Because I won't leave till you do.

Anna texted back.

Who is this?

She held her breath, hoping that somehow the reply would be different this time.

This is Lucy! Lucy Edwards!

Anna's hand shook as she typed.

That's impossible.

She was still stumped at who could be cruel enough to use Lucy's phone and send these messages. And now that her mom was gone, everything seemed even creepier.

Anna looked down at the phone and gasped.

Then I'll come to you.

Anna felt a sudden chill. This person had said the same thing before and nothing had happened. But it still freaked her out. This must be how those characters in horror movies felt when they got a phone call from a stalker saying "I can see you." If she were in a movie right now, what would she do?

The thought of hiding under her bed came to mind.

It was a hoax. A prank. That was all. Someone trying to scare her.

But just in case . . .

Anna crept over to the large living room window and peered through the blinds.

She blinked once. Twice. Her eyes had to be playing tricks on her, she thought. A girl was in her yard. Actually, at the end of the driveway. And she seemed to either be singing or talking to herself. She was too far away and the porch lights didn't help enough to see clearly, but she seemed harmless enough.

Anna felt as if she were watching a movie play out in front of her—this time a comedy—when the girl started making strange hand movements. Like she was signaling a plane. Then she bent down, stood up, yelled something, and started walking backward.

It looked as if this girl couldn't make up her mind. She walked forward two steps, back three. And for some reason, she was awfully interested in one of the bushes down there. Anna shook her head in wonder. And just like that, in the blink of an eye, the girl was gone.

Anna pressed her face to the glass. Had she imagined the girl? She'd seemed so real.

The doorbell rang, the tinkling of chimes echoing throughout the halls. Anna slammed her forehead against the window as she nearly jumped out of her skin. She was definitely on edge. Maybe she ought to cut out the caffeine.

She tiptoed to the door, afraid whoever it was would hear her inside, and looked through the peephole.

Nobody was there.

Until a sudden blue blob clouded her vision from the other side. A blue blob that almost looked like . . . an eyeball?

Anna screamed, jumping away from the door as if it were on fire. She ran back to the living room, looking for pieces of furniture that were big enough to hide under. When she failed, she grabbed the next best thing—a blanket folded over the back of the couch. She jumped in the rocker and threw the blanket over her body in one swoop.

The blood rushed to her head, and she could hear the swooshing of her heartbeat in her ears. Maybe she should call the cops. But what exactly would she say? Someone pretending to be a dead girl was texting her and someone knocked on her door but all she saw was an eyeball? Yeah, right. They would for sure think she was taking after Maxwell Maddsen.

It's this house, she thought. *It is* haunted!

She dug the phone out of her pocket, and giving in, she dialed her mom, who picked up on the first ring.

"Hello?"

"Hey, Mom."

"Hey, sweets. I didn't recognize the number. Where are you calling from?"

"It's a phone I found. On the way to school." Wow. It felt as if a thousand-pound weight had just been released from her shoulders.

"You *found* it?" Her mom sounded suspicious.

"No, I knocked over a cell phone store and this is what I have to show for it. Yes, Mom. I found it."

"Well, did you try—"

"I've already tried looking for the owner, yes. I'll give you every single deet later. That's not why I called." She heard her mom shushing someone before replying.

"Is everything okay? Are you hurt? Sick?"

Anna swallowed. "I'm fine." She didn't want to scare her mom—it wasn't like she could help her now anyway. But Anna felt better just hearing her voice.

There was a pause on the other end, and what sounded like a TV in the background. Anna picked at the wooden table with her fingernail, waiting for her mom to say something. The silence was making her nervous.

"I'm just doing hair and getting ready. You know how crazy it gets! Are you sure you're feeling all right, Annabel?"

"Yeah. I'm fine, really." Anna peered out from under the knit blanket, feeling pretty foolish. "I just called to, you know, see how it was going." She would sound crazy if she told her mom what was going on.

"Okay. Call me if you need anything. Promise?"

"I promise."

"All right, I have to go. I'll call you tomorrow. Love you, Annabel."

"Love you too, Mom."

The call disconnected. Feeling stuffy, Anna pulled

the blanket off her head, the static making her hair stick up. Replaying what had just happened, she was disappointed in herself. What had she been thinking? She feared for her life and chose to hide under a blanket? She could imagine the scene playing out in a horror movie. She, of course, played the main foolish character: "Oh, yes, a blanket will protect me from any crazy killers in the room!"

Still, she pulled the blanket around her shoulders.

And shivered.

CHAPTER 18

Lucy

Lucy had meant it when she'd said she would go to Anna if she refused to help her. And that was how she found herself standing in the long gravel road that led to Anna's house.

She only knew where Anna lived because she'd followed her home one day after school. Not like *stalking*-following—just following as in she happened to coincidentally go in the very same direction at the very same time, even though she couldn't remember where she was heading.

A sign at the head of the drive, now weathered and

missing letters, said MAD MANOR. The driveway was lined with huge, crooked oak trees. They resembled twisted, gnarled fingers reaching out of the ground. Spanish moss cascaded from the branches like water and swayed in the breeze.

Although the house looked like it had been abandoned forever, Lucy knew it wasn't. She caught glimpses of an old man rocking back and forth in a chair through the front window. She saw the shadow of a girl dancing in one of the rooms on the second floor, next to the window overlooking the front yard. Lucy could also feel an unexplainable connection to others inside who were hidden from sight.

Most of the property was overgrown, with vines covering the walls and even some of the first-floor windows. Wisteria dangled from a rusted iron gate. The dilapidated front porch held an old, broken swing and empty, cracked planters. She let her mind envision the swing fixed and new, and her sitting there, sipping a Red Bull and listening to the crickets at night. Maybe this place had potential. She'd have to make the best of a bad situation, since she planned to stick around for as long as it took to convince Anna to help her.

Lucy wished she could just go back home and pretend everything was fine. But her parents blamed each other for her accident, for not being around enough.

Lucy tried to tell them it wasn't their fault, but they couldn't hear her. They didn't even try. And when she wanted to comfort her mom, her arms went right through her.

And even though she heard her parents say the "D" word several times, Lucy refused to believe she was . . . well, she couldn't even say it. She couldn't accept something so crazy.

Also, she had unfinished business with John, and that would totally mess up her plans.

Lucy had watched her parents select their clothes for the funeral. It was too sad to think about. She'd whispered goodbye to them, but no one had heard her.

And then she was alone.

She'd walked down the long driveway to Mad Manor, the gravel crunching beneath her shoes, listening to the birds singing and the rustling of trees in the wind. From the corner of her eye, a shadow caught her attention, and she turned her head.

Nothing.

And then a noise from one of the bushes on her right.

She squinted against the sun, straining to see, and caught movement by the broken concrete next to an empty cherub fountain. Lucy crouched down, clutching her book bag to her chest like a shield, waiting for something to come blasting straight toward her.

Under the bush she saw a massive gray paw.

If she had still had functioning organs, her breath would've caught in her lungs at the exact moment she also tried to swallow the lump rising in her throat. This wasn't the paw of any animal she'd ever seen before. Probably not even an animal at all. This was an enormous creature.

Lucy was determined to stay strong and not be overcome by this monstrous . . . thing. She'd read enough in her fourteen years and considered herself very knowledgeable about vampires and werewolves. Nothing could shock her.

She took a deep breath and stood up straight, but the gray paw disappeared from her sight. A low hum sounded, and suddenly water began spurting and coughing from the fountain, the same fountain that looked as if it hadn't worked properly for hundreds of years. The water spit over the sides and into the bushes, flattening the leaves.

Two dark eyes were staring at her.

She could run like an awkward coward—since her legs seemed to be frozen in place—or stay and face a horrifying, tragic death. She shivered at the thought.

Mustering up every ounce of bravery she possessed, she took small steps forward.

The bush rumbled a little. Or was that her shaking?

"Come out now!" Lucy demanded, her fists balled up tightly at her sides.

Nothing.

Lucy's heart skipped several beats. Or it would've, if she'd had a heartbeat.

I'm not scared. Not scared at all. Lucy was certain that if she repeated the thought enough, she could convince herself it was true.

After she made a few coaxing sounds, she began to lose patience. "Fine, then!" she cried. "I'm coming in after you."

She marched straight over to the bush to show that beast who was boss and . . . peered down at a tattered mass of matted fur. It was just a cat, and it wasn't the least bit powerful or muscular. It was scrawny and bedraggled and not at all cute.

It was the poor, flat body of a kitty who had spent all of his nine lives.

Her fingertips itched to pet him. Fate must have brought their two lonesome souls together. Taking small steps, she got close enough to touch him. Up close, he was hideous. No animal should have had to suffer with such ugliness. She gradually lifted her hand and held it out to his fur.

With sweet, encouraging words, she let him know how lucky he was that she'd found him. Then she cautiously picked up the little beast. His body seemed stiff, a bit tense. And if she was completely honest, she'd have to say his fur felt like sandpaper.

"You, Mr. Roadkill Kitty, were meant to be found. From this day on, I will be yours and you will be mine. And I shall name you Pancake."

Cradling her new pet under one arm, Lucy walked up the creaky porch steps of the mansion and punched the doorbell.

She could feel Anna on the other side, lingering. Listening.

But the door never opened.

CHAPTER 19

ANNA

The following morning, Anna pushed open the large wooden door to the library, the faint scent of tobacco tickling her nose. She'd decided to grab a book to bring to school and read at lunch.

Although the room looked empty, it didn't feel that way. She threw herself into an oversized leather chair, scanning the hundreds of books lining the walls.

A book from the nearest shelf lingered on the edge before falling out, landing with a plop on the ground. Anna watched in amazement as another book flew off the shelf. It shot across the room and hit the wall with such force she almost expected to see an indentation.

And then it happened again. Book after book, each at a different speed, with different force. Anna closed her eyes, shaking her head. She hadn't slept well last night. This had to be a hallucination. She had to be imagining this.

There was no other explanation.

Anna's eyes snapped open just in time to see a book hurling straight at her head. She jumped to the floor just as the book hit the back of her chair, landing in her seat with a soft thud.

"Stop!" Anna had no idea why she yelled it, or who she thought she was yelling at, but it was as if she thought the one word would have enough power to suddenly stop the chaos.

And it did.

Anna's phone chimed with an incoming message.

I'll stop if you help me. Agreed?

Goose bumps prickled up her arms. Anna had a sudden urge to run from the house and never look back.

Thump.

Another book fell off the shelf, this time landing by her feet, the cover staring at her.

The Haunting of Hill House.

Another text message flashed on her phone.

I'm not going away.

As if to punctuate that last message, two more books flew at Anna, hitting her below the knees. She sucked in a sharp breath, sending a reply.

What do you want?

I want to know what happened.

How am I supposed to help you with that?

Talk to my boyfriend. He might know.

Why can't you talk to him?

Because he's ignoring me!

Who's your boyfriend?

John Butler. You have to talk to him! Let him know I'm OK! Well, not really OK, but I'm here and I miss him and . . . I need to know what happened!

I don't even know who this is.

I've told you! This is Lucy Edwards!

Anna squeezed the phone hard as she punched in the message.

Lucy is dead.

The texts stopped. Her phone remained silent.

The temperature in the room suddenly dropped. Anna rubbed her hands along her arms, teeth chattering.

Anna could see her breath in front of her.

The lights overhead flickered twice. Three times. She crinkled her nose as she suddenly caught a whiff of fresh lemon.

The books rose from the ground, slowly at first, hovering in place. Then they began to spin in a small circle around the room, a tornado of books. The air seemed to shimmer. Like magic, a transparent figure formed in front of her.

Two round blue eyes, framed by a familiar heart-shaped face, stared into hers.

It was the girl from the cafeteria. The girl from the yearbook picture.

It *was* Lucy.

Well, part of her. Other than her head, the rest of her was nearly transparent. Anna could see the entire room right through her. She jumped back as a scream tore through her throat.

Lucy's floating head bobbed up and down as she opened her mouth as if to scream as well, but no sound came out.

And then she was gone.

The temperature became warm. The lights stopped flickering. The books fell to the floor.

Anna crumpled into the chair, feeling limp and weak, as if every ounce of energy had been sucked straight out of her. She buried her head in her hands.

Her mind told her that logically, none of this had just happened.

Logically, there was no explanation. Other than maybe she was going crazy.

Like Great-Uncle Maddsen.

Anna stood, gently kicking the books aside as she made her way out of the room. She'd worry about the mess later.

One book in particular caught her eye. She bent down and picked up the worn leather-bound book tied up with string. She unwound the string and opened the pages. They were crisp and yellowed with age. Each page was filled with old-fashioned handwriting scrawled in black ink.

She turned back to the first page and read the first few lines.

I have not lost my mind. Everyone I know has turned against me. I am crazy, they say. No one will try to understand. Even my wife, Esther, thinks it to be

true. But I will prove them wrong. All of them. Even
if it takes me to my grave.

Anna gasped. This wasn't just any book. It was a diary.

And it belonged to Maxwell Maddsen.

CHAPTER 20

Lucy

Dead?

Lucy wasn't dead. She was looking at herself right now. That girl Anna didn't have a clue what she was talking about.

Lucy found herself suddenly back in the graveyard. Back where it all started. She felt so lost and out of control. Anna was the only person she was able to contact, and she refused to help.

With Pancake tucked under her arm, Lucy floated through the rows of headstones, head hanging low, arms limply at her sides. A feeling of depression

washed over her before disappearing as quickly as it had come. Being dead sounded so . . . permanent.

But maybe it didn't have to be. Maybe if she acted like everything was normal and she continued through the day as she always did, then nothing would change.

I am so brilliant, Lucy thought as she headed to Winchester Academy.

Once she was on school grounds, Lucy's mood deflated quickly. She had expected to feel different coming back to her school, since she had been away for so long. But as she floated down the halls, she still felt lost in a sea of faceless students. She was invisible. Forgotten. And no one spoke to her. But that was typical. She had always been the school nobody.

All the memories came flooding back: How she was socially awkward. How she was afraid of drawing attention to herself. How she'd been without a boyfriend only weeks before. Although to Lucy, it seemed more like a lifetime.

Caution: horribly sad, heart-wrenching tale ahead.

Lucy had sat in the back of her sixth-period classroom. Anxiety had closed her throat tight. Mrs. Chambers had just assigned partners on a project, and everyone was buddied up. Everyone but Lucy. Even her own teacher had forgotten about her.

Now Lucy had to draw attention to herself. She

slowly raised her hand, trying her best to control the trembling that usually came with speaking above a whisper in front of a group. Her hand hung there for several moments, making her heart race and shudder even more. Just as Lucy was about to have a full-blown seizure, Mrs. Chambers finally noticed.

"Ah, yes. Um . . . ," the teacher said, looking flustered.

Lucy sighed. It had been over a month since classes started and yet Mrs. Chambers still seemed shocked when she saw Lucy, like she was surprised there was suddenly an extra student in her class.

"It's Lucy," she said, straining to make her voice loud enough to be heard from her favorite seat in the very back, near the corner. A few people turned to look at her and Lucy lowered her eyes, hiding her face behind her hair. "You didn't assign me a partner."

Mrs. Chambers stared at her, then glanced down at her list, double-checking that Lucy wasn't just a figment of her imagination.

"Uh, you're right," she sputtered, a slight blush creeping over her gently wrinkled skin. "Would any team be interested in taking on another member?"

Lucy clenched her fists. This was going to be like dodgeball in sixth grade. Picked last. Every single time. Or maybe not at all.

There was a low murmur . . . but nobody volunteered. It stung, but Lucy tried to ignore it. Whatever. She had the brains to do the project on her own. Sure, it was a big project, but it wasn't like working on it would eat into her social life.

Lucy took a deep breath, trying to find the courage to muster a few more words and tell Mrs. Chambers that she would be happy working alone. . . .

Then a single hand shot up, straight and confident, from the middle of the room. Lucy couldn't see who it belonged to.

"Johnny?" Mrs. Chambers said, recognizing the hand's owner instantly. Johnny must be the memorable type.

"We'll do it," he said.

"Thank you, Johnny." Mrs. Chambers nearly sang the words as she beamed at him, like a huge weight had been lifted from her shoulders. "That makes my life much easier!"

Lucy scowled from behind her curtain of hair. *Easier?* Was she really that much of a burden?

"Now, the assignment will be due next month. You will be getting class time to work on this, but—"

The bell rang, cutting the teacher's explanation short. People began gathering their things and spilling into the hallway.

As Lucy left the room, a boy was leaning casually against the wall next to the door. "Hey," he said, smiling at her.

She realized it was the boy who'd volunteered to work with her. "Hi," Lucy said, with no idea what else to say.

There was an awkward pause. Lucy didn't know if he was waiting for her to say something, but she didn't.

He laughed, breaking the silence. Usually, if someone laughed at Lucy—because she was too dorky or she studied too much—she would turn and flee. But there was a brightness in Johnny's eyes that made it obvious he wasn't laughing *at* her. And he actually seemed a little . . . nervous.

"Hope you don't mind you're part of our group now," he said as he glanced down the hall and frowned a little. He looked back at Lucy and shrugged. "I guess Nessa had to get to her class quickly or something."

Lucy nodded. He was really cute.

After lingering for another moment, Lucy kept waiting for him to suddenly notice what a loser she was and make some excuse to escape from her presence. She expected him to realize that he shouldn't be wasting his time talking to her. She was nowhere near close to his social level. Not even close to existing in the same universe. Like if you took a soggy pickle (her) and a prime rib. Those two would never be caught dead on the same plate. Ever.

But he didn't notice. Who she was didn't seem to bother him.

"So, let's exchange information," Johnny said, tearing off a corner of a page from his notebook. He scribbled his phone number on it and handed it to her. "Text me whenever."

"Okay," she said quietly, stuffing the paper in her pocket. "I'll text you my number." She started to inch away from him. She couldn't remember the last time she'd talked to a cute guy. Oh, right, it was never.

He gave her a nod. "Okay. Later."

Maybe this partner project wouldn't be so bad after all, Lucy decided as she watched him go. And it was at that precise moment she knew.

She was in love.

CHAPTER 21

ANNA

Anna had never been to a funeral before, but she imagined they were all pretty much like this one. It was cloudy and drizzling, the perfect weather for a tragedy. It seemed everyone from school was here, probably just to get out of class early. Except Olivia. She had come down with a sudden "migraine" and gone home.

All around Anna, people patted their dry eyes with

tissues and talked in hushed whispers. In front of her . . . well, she wanted to avoid looking at the creepy coffin. Just knowing that someone was inside threatened to give her nightmares.

Anna felt the phone in her coat pocket vibrating. She waited for it to stop, but it didn't. Her mom had said it was okay to buy a new battery, and now it seemed to work better than ever. She pulled her coat tighter and glanced around the crowd. Nobody was paying any attention to her. She turned and slipped away without being noticed.

Her shoes sank into the damp grass with every step until she reached a large tree. Leaning against the trunk and facing away from everyone, she pulled out her phone.

18 new text messages.

"What the heck?" She scrolled through the messages, all from unknown or blocked numbers, except one. None of them seemed to make any sense. Until she got to one from a number she did recognize.

Lucy Edwards's. The text read:

Nice funeral. Olivia's?

Why was someone still using Lucy's phone? That was just creepy.

> Just gonna stare at your phone and not
> answer?

A paranoid feeling swept through Anna as she looked behind her. It was probably one of Olivia's friends playing a trick.

> I bet you won't miss Olivia either, right?

Anna's finger trembled as she typed.

> What are you talking about????
> Why won't you help me?

Anna rolled her eyes. She was so over having this conversation again.

> Fine. I'll just come visit you again. I'm getting better, you know.

Anna texted back.

> What do you mean, again????
> Remember that floating head in your library?
> Yeah, that was me.

Anna gulped. Floating head? No. That was a hallucination. She hadn't told anyone about it.

> I even flashed the lights. Three times! Do you
> know how exhausting that was?

Anna shook her head. "No. That stuff wasn't real," she whispered.

> I don't know what you're talking about, Anna
> texted back.

> C'mon! The flying books? I even surprised
> myself! Give me some credit for my effort!

Not possible. Anna's knuckles turned white as she held her phone in a death grip. Just then another text message popped up. This time from another unknown number.

> You just knocked over my flowers. Mind
> picking them up?

Anna's head snapped up. She had wandered away from the tree. Glancing down, she noticed a vase with dried-up flowers at her feet. She propped the vase up against the headstone, then quickly backed away, her eyes darting from her phone to the grave.

"Lucy" texted again.

> Please, Anna! Help me. Don't make me beg!
> You were so nice to me that day at lunch when
> we exchanged numbers. You even made me
> feel better about the mean kids staring. You
> weren't like them.

The phone shook in Anna's hands. Was this really happening?

> And even when I told you to leave the lunch
> table, you said you would stay and take your
> chances.

"Lucy?" Anna whispered.

> In the flesh. Well, kind of.

She took a long, deep breath, letting it out slowly. "It's true," she whispered. "I can text dead people."

CHAPTER 22

Lucy

Lucy settled against the school wall the next day, waiting outside John's class. She had stuffed Pancake in her bag since he was getting heavy, even though he didn't quite fit. Throwing her hair over her shoulder,

she reached into her bag, maneuvering around the cat, and pulled out some of her schoolbooks. She really didn't have to study anymore, since technically she was no longer a student. But going through the motions made her feel more . . . normal.

As John came around the corner, Lucy meant to walk up to him. But instead, she swooshed past him. She turned and hurried back.

"Hi," she said, feeling nervous. She held her books tightly against her chest, afraid the pounding of her heart might be visible through her shirt.

"Hey," he said, a smile spreading across his face.

She beamed back at him.

"Hey, Johnny," a voice said behind Lucy. Lucy whipped around, facing the wide smile of a beautiful girl.

It was Eden Ashbury. Lucy realized Johnny wasn't talking *to* her, but *through* her.

Lucy scowled at Eden. "Back off."

Saying Eden was pretty was an understatement. It was like saying the sky was blue or water is wet. She had huge blue eyes and long, straight ice-blond hair, and it all seemed to be in perfect balance with her pale skin and delicate pixie-like features.

Lucy's anxiety flared, her gaze lingering on Eden a bit too long. She was unable to handle the concept of the two of them talking to each other.

"Johnny," Eden said, sidling up beside him, gently touching his arm. "Are you going to walk me home today?"

Johnny's cheeks went slightly pink, something Lucy had never seen before. He was always composed. Except for the day he'd met her outside the classroom and given her his phone number.

Somehow, this girl made him blush. Of course, it

wasn't surprising, since she was so beautiful. And popular. Lucy's stomach became hot and heavy, like someone had dropped a glob of molten lava down her throat.

"Uh, yeah. Sure," John stammered, something else Lucy had never seen him do. Eden had really flustered him.

Eden's mouth twitched into a small smile. "Great. Meet me here after school." Her voice sounded like tinkling bells.

Lucy's chest felt tight and her knees wobbled. She slunk off in the other direction, heading toward her next class.

In the days that followed, John failed to wave or say hi to Lucy in the halls. She watched him across the crowded halls on breaks or across the street after school. If he saw her, he gave no indication. Sometimes, if they ran into each other at the right moment, John would give a shudder and run his hands up his goose-bumped arms. Maybe she could make him see her again. Notice her.

Deep down, Lucy knew the truth. But for the first time in forever, she hoped for something. She wanted something. And it was something money couldn't buy. Lucy raced to Anna's house, more eager for her help than ever. Maybe everything could finally go back to normal.

Because the more Lucy watched Johnny, seeing him with his friends, with strangers, with anyone— the more she realized that he treated her just the way he treated everyone. She wasn't special. He genuinely cared for people. He was just that way, just . . . nice.

But Lucy couldn't let it go. She couldn't stop liking him. He had turned on a switch inside her that she couldn't turn off.

Lucy loved him. And she would always love him.

Even after her last pathetic breath.

CHAPTER 23

ANNA

"A what?" Lucy laughed, petting Pancake's head.

"A ghost," Anna explained. "Like a spirit. You know, dead." Where was that lemon smell coming from?

"But—" Lucy's head darted side to side like a hard-hit Ping-Pong ball.

"I know this is hard for you to accept. But you're a ghost. You tripped and hit your head in the cemetery. Don't you remember?"

Lucy touched her head. "It feels fine." Her fingers brushed against an egg-sized lump.

"You do all the things only

156

ghosts can do, including disappearing anytime you want."

Lucy nearly laughed. "And walking through walls?" she asked sarcastically.

Anna huffed. "Whether you like it or not, *you are a ghost*. And in case you haven't noticed, you float." Anna pointed at Lucy's feet, which hovered a few inches above the ground.

Lucy looked down. Anna was right—she was floating! People couldn't float. Only ghosts could. That meant . . .

No.

Her newfound fate hit her like a wrecking ball. She was a ghost! Lucy scrambled, trying not to fall. She'd never been a ghost before. She could hardly believe it. She crushed the cat to her chest. "How?" Her bottom lip quivered. "How did it happen?"

"In the cemetery. We just went over that part. Did you forget already?"

"The cemetery?" Lucy's brain felt completely scrambled.

"So why were you in the cemetery that night?"

"That night . . . I was supposed to meet John, and . . . and I remember some kind of bright light. I woke up in the cemetery. But—"

"You didn't really wake up. You were already gone."

Lucy's face crumpled as if she were about to cry, but her eyes were completely dry. Anna wondered if it was even possible for a ghost to cry.

"Wait . . . did you say you were meeting Johnny that night?"

Lucy nodded. "Yeah. Why?"

"He was at the Ashbury party. He said after your accident that he wished he had texted you back."

"But he did text me back. Look." Lucy held her phone out for Anna to see the message.

That's okay. See you soon. It was from Johnny, but that didn't seem right. Anna had never seen him leave the party. And why would he text Lucy that?

"So that's it, then. I'm really dead." Lucy's voice quavered, and Anna almost wanted to give her a hug. Almost. She would need more time before she could go around actually touching dead people.

"Yeah, I'm sorry. Your parents were never ignoring you. It's just that nobody can hear you. Or see you."

"Then how can you?"

Anna shrugged. "I must be cursed." *Or going crazy like my great-uncle,* she silently added.

"A curse? Don't tell me you actually believe in witches!" Lucy laid Pancake back in her lap, petting him slowly from head to tail. "Since you're the only one I can talk to, you're the only one who can help me figure out what really happened that night."

Anna nodded.

"And help me see my boyfriend again."

"Um . . ." Anna didn't think that was such a great idea, but she also didn't want Lucy haunting her forever. That would make her teen years really awkward. "Fine. Okay. But after that, this ghost business is done."

"Deal. And one more thing."

"What's that?"

"I don't like the word 'ghost.' Use something else."

"How about 'pain in my butt'?" Anna muttered under her breath.

. . .

Lucy transported herself back to the graveyard, hugging her shoulders, chin tight to her chest. She felt hollow. Alone. Was this how it would always feel now that she was a gh—spirit? Lucy twisted a lock of her hair. She had no family. No friends, unless she counted Anna. And now no way to see Johnny. Sure, Anna had agreed to talk to him for her, but until then, what would she do every day? It already seemed like an eternity.

"At least I have you, Pancake." She held the unresponsive cat close, blinking back tears. "It's okay. I feel the love."

It wouldn't be as bad if she at least knew what to expect. Those people in *Beetlejuice* had it way easier than her. They at least had their *Handbook for the Recently Deceased*.

As it started to get dark, Lucy still floated without direction, her mind spinning at a hundred miles per hour. Her emotions seesawed more than a first grader at recess. What did it matter what she did or didn't do now? There was no point to anything, no life to live.

Lucy stared straight ahead, a bleak look on her face. She wanted to sleep for the rest of the day. Or even through this whole ghostly nonexistence thing. Then she wouldn't have to think about it. Or feel anything.

She searched for a place to rest. It wasn't like she could sleep in a human bed anymore. She had no idea, as a newborn spirit, how this was supposed to work. Should she just find a fresh mound of dirt in the cemetery? Or maybe a coffin?

A coffin sounded much more inviting. No, not the occupied ones six feet under. Dead people still creeped her out. But the funeral home was only a few yards away. They would be sure to have a display room with an assortment of comfy coffins.

Lucy chose the first coffin she laid eyes on, not even caring that it wasn't the most expensive. Or that it was so last season.

And then, closing her eyes, she fell into a deep, ghostly sleep.

. . .

Anna was barely awake, so she only noticed Spencer standing at her locker the next morning when she was a few steps from it. Her stomach flipped nervously. She hesitated, then walked toward him cautiously.

"Hi," she said as she twisted the dial of the lock.

"I need to talk to you," Spencer said, almost whispering.

"About what?" Anna asked, opening her locker, relieved to not find a new surprise left for her.

"About Lucy Edwards."

Anna looked directly at Spencer. "What about her?"

"I don't feel comfortable talking about it here," Spencer said. "Can you meet me after school? In the yearbook room? I have a class there last period and the teacher likes me. He'll let me stay if I tell him I need to finish a project."

"I don't know." Anna felt unsure about this meeting. If Spencer was the one who had left that picture of Lucy in her book, then he had probably put the rose in her locker too. She still didn't know why, but she wasn't sure she wanted to find out.

"Please. I really need to talk to you," Spencer said.

Anna sighed. "Okay."

. . .

After school Anna hurried toward the yearbook room. The school had emptied out. Her footsteps echoed eerily down the hallway.

The door opened into a classroom with only a dozen or so desks, and a brown leather couch up against the far wall. The bright fluorescent lights flickered and hummed above her.

"Spencer?" Anna said as she stepped inside. "Are you here?" She walked in a little farther.

There was another door at the back of the classroom. "Spencer?" she called again.

There was no answer, only silence. Anna walked to the door and pushed it open. "Spencer?" she tried again, entering a small, dimly lit room. The door automatically shut behind her. Spencer wasn't there. It was empty. Anna felt a chill crawl up her spine as she looked at pictures lying on one of the shelves. She realized Spencer must've taken them.

It was obvious that Spencer wasn't showing up. Anna turned to open the door, when she noticed a backpack lying on the ground next to a stack of papers. Maybe it was Spencer's, she thought; maybe he had just run to the restroom. She wouldn't know if it was his unless she opened it, she reasoned. As she bent down to unzip the backpack, she felt a twinge of guilt but pushed it away. She would wait for him if the backpack was his, but otherwise she wanted to get out of this room.

The bag opened, revealing the usual set of books and notebooks. She pulled out a notebook and looked at the inside cover, where Spencer's name was written in cramped, scribbled letters. She shut the notebook and put it back in the backpack before she was tempted to look through it any further. As she stood up, one of the photo prints caught her eye and she moved closer to get a better look in the dim light.

There was a picture of Lucy, smiling. It was different from the photo Anna had found in her book. In this photo, Lucy was wearing an outfit that Anna recognized. It was the outfit Lucy still wore now. It was what she wore the night she became a spirit.

The night she . . . died.

Anna felt a chill crawl up her spine. She felt goose bumps on her arms. Suddenly it didn't matter if Spencer was coming back to meet her or not. Anna wanted nothing more than to get out of there. She rushed back toward the door, pushing against it with all her might.

It didn't move.

Anna pushed harder.

Nothing happened. The door wasn't budging. She stepped back a few feet and ran at the door as hard as she could. It didn't move an inch. She ran again, panic taking hold, and threw her shoulder full force into the door. She fell to the floor, holding her right shoulder, which throbbed in pain.

"Help! I'm stuck in here!" Anna yelled as loudly as she could.

Even as she did, though, the thought that no one would find her until morning ran through her mind. She had gotten locked in somehow. A frightening notion took hold of her: what if someone had purposely locked her in? But why? Was she in danger? She looked around the room. There was nothing dangerous in there. She doubted she'd die before morning. Still, her brain was in full panic mode. She had to get out of there. She was beginning to feel as if she was using up all the air in the room. She pulled out her phone. There were no bars. She tried calling Millie. Nothing happened. She moved to another corner of the room and tried again.

Nothing.

She walked around the room holding the phone, looking for reception. It was useless. What was she going to do? She put the phone back in her pocket and listened for any sounds coming from the other room.

There was only silence. She waited one minute and then another, scanning the small room for something to help her escape.

She didn't know how thick the door was—maybe it was so thick that she wouldn't even hear someone on the other side, and they wouldn't hear her. Fear rose in her throat at the realization of her situation.

"Help!" Anna cried again, unable to stay silent.

She wasn't normally claustrophobic, but the thought of spending the night in the tiny, cramped space frightened her. Anna took a deep breath. She had to stay calm. *Think,* she told herself, *you have to think.* She started pacing back and forth. Her thoughts were racing so much it was hard to focus. She didn't know what to do.

Besides, if someone had locked her in, they could come back in the middle of the night and get her. It was terrifying.

Then she remembered the shelf near Spencer's backpack. There was more than one picture there, and Anna looked closely at all of them. There were eight shots of the party. Anna didn't recognize the people in most of them, but some were familiar. One of them showed Eden laughing. Someone was in the background . . . in jeans, a black hoodie, and mud-coated sneakers.

Another picture was of Anna near the snack table.

And although Millie should've been somewhere in the background, she wasn't.

It was a good picture of her, Anna thought, although she also thought she looked a little lost and lonely. That meant that Spencer had been watching her that night.

The sound of the scraping against the door brought Anna immediately out of her thoughts. Terror surged through her body. A cold sweat broke out over her skin. There were no weapons within reach. Unless you counted a stapler.

Anna swung her bag onto one shoulder, prepared to swing it at whoever was coming into the room.

Everything seemed to happen in slow motion.

The doorknob seemed to turn forever as Anna waited to see who was there. She saw a hand and a flash of a gray shirt.

And then she swung her bag with all her might.

CHAPTER 24

ANNA

Anna felt her messenger bag connect with the person. He doubled over, clutching the bag to his stomach as it knocked him to the floor. She had been hoping to see his face, but there was no time to waste. This was her chance. She bolted for the door.

As Anna ran past him, he managed to grab the hem of her jeans. She struggled against him, kicking like crazy, finally connecting hard enough so that he grunted in pain and let go.

Anna pushed at the door in blind panic.

"Anna! It's me, Spencer!"

Anna hesitated, hands against the wood, seconds from free-dom. Should she trust him?

"C'mon. I didn't mean to scare you," Spencer said, sitting up. He clutched the side of his mouth, where, Anna realized, she had kicked him.

She turned toward him, hoping she was making the right decision. She sat down next to him and peered at his face in the dim light. "Are you okay? I'm sorry I kicked you. I got locked in here somehow and I didn't know if you were coming in here to kill me or something."

He gave her a strange look. "Why would I come in here to kill you? I had to run to my locker for a second and figured I'd be back in time to meet up with you. One of my teachers stopped me in the hall, though, and that's why I was late."

"Someone locked me in here," Anna said, trying to breathe normally.

Spencer nodded. "I know. There was a chair wedged under the doorknob. I thought you decided not to show. But then I saw the chair. Why would someone do that?"

"I don't know." Anna stared at the floor. Then, before she could stop herself, Anna was telling him the story of the rose in her locker, the yearbook photo in her textbook. And then she told him about Lucy. She felt herself relaxing a bit after blurting out so much, but she figured she didn't know him well, so if he thought she was crazy, then who cared? And if he decided to tell everyone, then she'd deal with it.

"That's pretty crazy," he said when she was finished.

"I know! I thought I was losing my mind. But I'm not. It's all real. I don't know how, but it is," Anna said, putting her head in her hands.

"I know it's real," Spencer said. "I think Lucy's been haunting me too. Every night around midnight I'm woken up by freaky, unexplainable things happening."

Anna looked up. "Really?" A sentence from Maxwell's journal came to mind: *Midnight till one: it belongs to the dead*.

"Yeah. And I think I know why," Spencer said glumly.

"Does it have anything to do with the photo you took of her? It's from that night, isn't it?" she asked.

"Yeah," Spencer said. "And I think she believes I know what happened that night."

"Do you?" Anna asked, staring at him.

Spencer sighed. "I know she went to the cemetery that night to meet Johnny."

"But why?" It didn't make sense.

Spencer ran a hand through his hair. "I think someone pretended to be Johnny and told her to meet him there."

"What?" Anna was stunned.

Spencer sighed again. "I was outside taking pictures.

Someone came out of the Ashbury house in jeans and a black hoodie."

Anna's mind was whirling. "Who do you think it was?"

"I'm not sure, but I followed them to the cemetery. And I happened to snap a photo of Lucy right before it all happened," Spencer told her. "But that's it. That's all I know. But she won't leave me alone."

"Wow," Anna said. "I'll talk to her, but . . . just curious, why did you want to talk to me about Lucy in the first place?"

Spencer shrugged. "I saw you sitting with her in the cafeteria that day. She never really talked to anyone around school, so I thought maybe she was visiting you too."

Anna laughed. "Good guess."

• • •

It was Saturday morning. Anna stared out the window at the falling rain, her hands wrapped around a warm mug of hot chocolate. The tinkling of the bell sounded every time someone entered or left the Corner Café, which seemed to be every ten seconds. Her stomach growled at the smell of fresh cinnamon rolls and buttery biscuits.

Her phone vibrated in her pocket. She pulled it out and checked the message.

Have you talked to him yet?

It was Lucy. Again.
Anna frowned.

I will. I am!

Finally!

Anna tugged on the edge of her beige knitted beanie, pulling it down farther until it touched the tips of her lashes. Her straight hair was already frizzing from the moisture, and her cheeks were pink from the cold morning air.

The door opened and Johnny walked in. "Hey," he said, brushing some droplets from his jacket. He got a doughnut and mug of warm milk, then pulled up a chair and sat next to her.

"Thanks for meeting me," Anna said. "I have a question for you." There was no use beating around the bush.

"Shoot." Johnny took a sip from his mug.

Anna decided to feel him out. "So, Johnny . . . let's say hypothetically you were being haunted."

Johnny gave her a funny look. "Ghosts?"

"Well, yeah. Like when someone dies, don't you think they might hang around for a while after?"

Johnny bit into his doughnut. "Uh, no, I don't really believe in that kind of stuff."

"I used to be that way," Anna said as her phone started to vibrate. "But I'm trying to be more open-minded now." She tucked her hair behind her ear, ignoring the phone. "I was wondering . . . I know you said you don't have a girlfriend, but—"

He set his cup down. "You're not jealous of Eden, are you? Because if you were, that would be totally cool too."

"Eden's your girlfriend?" Anna asked, surprised. She hadn't expected that.

Johnny shook his head, laughing. "No, but she's fun to hang out with."

"Like Lucy Edwards was?" Anna blurted out.

Johnny sighed. "Lucy and I weren't even friends. I barely knew her. Why are you so curious about a dead girl?"

"I guess being new here, I'm just trying to figure everything out," Anna said, taking a sip of her hot chocolate. Her phone buzzed again.

Did you talk to him about me yet??

No, she texted back. **Stop texting me!**

"I'm gonna get another doughnut," Johnny said, getting up. "You want one?"

Anna shook her head.

She had to tell Lucy the truth. Johnny had never cared about her at all. Alive or dead.

CHAPTER 25

ANNA

Anna was dying to tell Millie about her phone. About Lucy. But she doubted Millie would respond the way Spencer had. It wasn't likely she'd had a run-in with ghosts too.

She had played out several different scenarios in her head on how Millie might react to her news.

POSSIBLE REACTION #1
Anna: Hey, guess what? Ghosts are texting me.
Millie: *jaw drops*

POSSIBLE REACTION #2

Anna: Hey, guess what? I talk to dead people.

Millie: *rolls eyes* Yeah, right.

POSSIBLE REACTION #3

Anna: Hey, guess what? I communicate with the unliving.

Millie: What? You're crazy! *runs for the hills*

But even though Anna was pretty positive she had prepared herself for every outcome, she was dead wrong.

This is how it went down.

Anna: So . . . I am, I mean . . . I can, uh . . . there are things . . .

Millie: Just spit it out.

Anna: Okay, so don't freak, but . . .

Millie: Well, now I'm gonna freak. You can't start off by telling me not to.

Anna: Well, I can kinda maybe sorta communicate with things. Like ghosts.

Millie: Shut the front door!

Anna: Huh?

Millie: That is unbelievable!

Anna: I knew you weren't going to belie—

Millie: Awesome! So what are they saying?

Anna: You believe me?

Millie: Of course! I totally believe in stuff like that.

So telling Millie had been the easy part.

Now came the hard part: telling Lucy about Johnny.

She met with Lucy face to ghost on the porch steps of the Manor, hoping to break the news gently.

"What did you find out?" Lucy wrung her ghostly hands together.

Anna took a deep breath. "I . . . don't think Johnny—"

"John," Lucy corrected.

"Fine. I don't think John was ever really your boyfriend."

Lucy waved a hand dismissively. "I'm not interested in what *you* think. What did *he* say?"

"He said you were never his girlfriend. Maybe you got the wrong idea somehow and—"

"But he visited me a few days ago!"

Anna gave her a reproachful look. "You mean at your funeral?"

"And he brought me flowers," Lucy went on stubbornly. "My favorite kind."

"For your grave. And I was the one who suggested daisies, because I know you love daisies, remember?"

"But I gave him my heart!"

"I know you're going through so much right now, but—"

"No, really." Lucy pointed to her chest. "I *gave* him my heart. I think you should tell him to give it back until he's done acting this way."

Anna shook her head. "You're exhausting, you know that? So how's the haunting coming along? I've heard what you've been doing to Spencer. He doesn't know any more than we do, you know."

Lucy sighed. "I'm still learning the ropes of haunting people."

"People?" Anna repeated. "Who else are you haunting?"

Lucy gave a small shrug. "John. Eden. Olivia."

"Seriously?" Anna thought this was a bad idea. "Eden is nice; you need to leave her alone. And you shouldn't be messing with Olivia."

"Well, I only haunted Olivia for like a minute, so that shouldn't count. But you might be interested to know what I overheard."

"Haunting *and* eavesdropping?"

"Whatever. So Olivia was talking on her phone—don't ask me with who, because I have no idea—and she sounded super angry. She asked this person how they could be stupid enough to lose their phone."

"No way! Is that the phone I found?"

"I'm not done talking. She also told this person that she *did* try to find out if Anna—that's you—found the phone and it wasn't her fault that Anna—that's you again—lied to her. She said she did exactly what she was supposed to do and acted nice until she got the info and then dropped her duty. I'm guessing that's also you."

"Why wouldn't she just tell me someone lost their phone and ask if I had seen it?"

"Probably because there was something on the phone that they didn't want traced back to them."

"What makes you think that?"

"Because she said that too."

"Oh. But there wasn't really anything on the phone."

"Not my problem. But let me tell you what I found out about Eden," Lucy said, her face whitening in excitement. "Get this. . . . As it turns out, she's kind of a fan of all things . . . dead."

"Meaning what?"

"Have you seen that girl's room? It's like death threw up in there! Black wilted roses, black walls, and bleeding-heart posters. I think this girl might be a little, well . . . *off*."

"Really?" Anna asked, wrinkling her nose. She couldn't picture it. "But she's just so . . . pink."

"I'm serious. She has this other side to her. Trust me, her bedroom doesn't lie."

"She wasn't actually able to see you, right?" Anna asked.

"No, of course not. You're the only one special enough to do that," Lucy threw back sarcastically. "But she could definitely sense I was there. And then she thought it was all a big game and took out a huge book, and then—"

"And then?"

"And then she tried to cast a spell on me," Lucy said.

"She's a *witch*?"

"I don't know if she's a *real* witch—I mean, putting personality aside—but I've never really met one before, so how would I know? It's not like I checked her closet for a broom." Lucy shrugged. "I guess we'll know for sure if I grow a third head or something."

"Right. Because growing a second head would be so completely normal," Anna muttered.

CHAPTER 26

ANNA

Anytime a sentence starts with "There's something you need to know," that *something* is never good. So when Anna's mom said this while grabbing her hand and making her sit on the sofa with her, Anna knew it was the kind of bad that was impossible to take standing up. There was never any sit-down news that was good either.

"I have some news," her mom began.

"Just tell me already, Mom," Anna said.

"I got another job. Just something extra to do on the side, around my schedule at the salon. I'm working for Winston."

Anna stared at her. "The mortician guy? Doing what?"

Her mom cleared her throat. "Maybe I should just show you. It might be easier for you to accept."

"Show me what?" Anna eyed her mom suspiciously, not quite sure what she was up to.

Her mom reached for her hand and pulled her up from the couch. "Come on, let's go."

"Where are we going?" Anna asked as she followed her mom outside.

"The mortuary."

Anna stopped walking. "Okay, that's just . . . creepy."

"It's not that creepy."

Anna wasn't exactly one to talk. After all, texting dead people wasn't exactly *uncreepy*.

They walked around the corner from the Manor to Leavitt Funeral Home. Ms. Craven shivered from the cold as she rang the bell on the back door.

The outside porch light flickered a few times, and then the door slowly squeaked open.

Anna's mom pushed the door open and stuck her head inside. "Winston?"

The fluorescent lights buzzed loudly, sounding like

a hive of bees, before finally lighting up the small, windowless room. Its walls were stark white and the floor was tiled. There was a card table in the center that held an ashtray filled to the top with cigarette butts and an open, half-empty box of doughnuts, probably from the morning and stale. On the counter running along the side wall there was nothing but a coffeepot, an empty cup, and a microwave. *This must be where morticians take their coffee breaks*, Anna thought. The place gave her the creeps already.

"He's probably in his office," her mom said as they walked down a hallway. "Come on."

When they reached Winston's office, her mom went inside. Anna took a cone-shaped paper cup and filled it at the water cooler.

They'll probably be a while, she thought. She decided to take a look around.

As she walked down the hallway, a shudder went through her, followed by a buzz from her phone. And then another. And another. Anna pulled out her phone. The text messages were coming at lightning speed, too fast for her to even look at one message before another came in. Anna had to wait several minutes for the phone to calm down before she could read anything. Her jaw dropped as she scrolled through the first few.

Need help! Where am I?

I think I died. Can you help?

I shouldn't be here! It should be my sister!!

Where are my shoes?

She slowly walked backward, her eyes growing wider with each message. "Ouch!" She turned around, having bumped hard into a metal door behind her. A sign on it read MORGUE.

Anna wondered if there was a connection. Were the messages coming from inside that room? The signal on her phone was at full strength—something that happened any time she was close to a spirit. Anna searched the hallway, making sure her mom wasn't near, before turning the doorknob.

Anna gasped. It was a room full of Lucys. The place was crawling with spirits, all on ghostly cell phones. Each spirit looked more disgruntled than the one before, not that she could blame them. Luckily, none of them noticed her. She backed out, closing the door quietly until it softly clicked shut. She clutched her phone, which was still vibrating with incoming texts, and noticed that the screen was glowing super bright, as if the spirits could sense she was near and were controlling the phone.

And contacting me. Allowing me to communicate with them.

Anna ran down the hallway as if her life depended on it.

She stopped, gasping, outside a room filled with chairs and vases of flowers—and an open coffin. She walked closer until she could see a person in the ivory-silk-lined coffin. Her legs seemed to move on their own, until she was looking down at an older, balding man, his few gray strands of hair brushed to the side. Makeup had been applied to his skin in a really bad attempt to bring color to his cheeks. He wore a brown suit with matching silk tie, and Anna saw the hint of a smile on his lips.

Anna had never been this close to a corpse before.

She had the urge to touch the body. Would it dent if she poked it, like a stress ball? Or would it jiggle like jelly? Or maybe it would be stone hard and cold, like a statue. She hadn't the slightest idea, but she wanted to find out. Anna quickly looked behind her; then, with one finger, she reached down and . . .

"Eww!" she cried, zipping her hand away from the dead man's face. It felt like a ripe, unpeeled mango. She couldn't believe she had just done that. What was she thinking? Her phone started going off again.

Great, she thought, *it's probably his spirit texting to*

tell me off for doing that. She didn't bother checking the message.

Her mom and a man with a fuzzy black mustache—Winston, she guessed—came into the room. "Anna, this is Mr. Doombrowski," her mom said.

Anna gave him a weak smile. *More like Mr. Doom,* she thought. She was more than ready to leave.

"Now, where . . . did I put . . ." Winston patted down his pockets, searching for something. "I think I left it in the other room. Let's stop by there on the way out."

They turned off the lights as they went. "Think I left my phone in here—the embalming room." Winston unlocked a door on their right and entered, leaving Anna and her mother in the hallway.

Anna peeked into the embalming room. The pungent odor of formaldehyde and bleach wafted past her nose. It looked like a hospital room, with its sterile supply tray and fluorescent lighting and neatly ordered supplies lining the counters. Set into the far wall was the massive stainless-steel door to what looked like a walk-in refrigerator.

In the middle of the room, a girl lay on a metal table, a white sheet covering her body so that only her head was visible. Her face was free of makeup and her skin had a flat, chalky pallor. Her eyes were shockingly open, her mouth slightly parted, as if she were begging for another breath.

Anna's mom pulled her away from the door. "Don't look in there, honey."

Winston walked out briskly, closing the door behind him.

"I'm sorry," he apologized. "I'm not used to having anyone back here."

"It's okay." But it wasn't. Anna didn't think she could get the image of that girl out of her mind. She looked so unnatural, so strangely fake.

Anna's mom put her arm around her. "Seeing dead people can be pretty upsetting. That's why Winston hired me." She smiled. "I'm going to do their hair and makeup."

Anna considered this. "Well, if anyone can make her look the way she was, I know you can."

Her mom squeezed her shoulders. "Thanks, honey. That's really sweet of you."

Anna took a deep breath. Her mom was a corpse cosmetologist.

And Anna was never going to escape dead people.

CHAPTER 27

ANNA

A little while later, Anna popped her phone into her hoodie pocket, watching as her mom put the final touches on a woman in the funeral home's prep room. The body really did look fabulous. Her skin looked smooth and creamy. And she looked so peaceful, as if she were just taking a nap and would wake up any moment.

"What do you think?" her mom asked, taking a step back and examining her work.

"You did great, Mom. Really." She was a natural talent.

"Do you think she needs more lipstick? Or what about eyeliner?"

"You really need to learn when to stop fussing," Anna laughed.

"Anna?"

She spun around to see Olivia standing in the doorway. Anna walked over to her. "What are you doing here?" she asked in hushed whisper.

Olivia furrowed her brows. "It's a funeral home. Take a guess."

"Right, I just mean did someone you know—"

"No, nothing like that. My grandma's name was misspelled on her gravestone, so we're just sorting it out." She rolled her eyes like it was a huge inconvenience. "So . . . your mom dresses dead people."

"She doesn't *dress* them." What an idiot. "She's a cosmetologist."

"Same thing. Whatever, I don't care. Just don't mention to anyone that you saw me here today, okay?"

Anna stared at her. "Why?"

"Does it really matter? Just don't say anything."

Anna shrugged. "Fine. As long as you don't say anything to anyone either."

"Fine," Olivia tossed off over her shoulder as she walked away.

"Ready to go?" Anna's mom appeared, holding a

makeup bag under her arm. "Just got to give this to Winston first."

They found Winston back in the break room, eating a tuna salad sandwich. How anyone could have an appetite in a place like this was beyond Anna.

Her mom handed Winston the makeup bag. "We're taking off now."

Winston nodded, wiping his mouth with a napkin. "Thank you for helping out today."

"Did you just have a family in here?" Anna couldn't help but ask.

"Nope, not today."

"Nobody? Not even to fix a misspelled gravestone?"

Winston snorted, almost spitting out bits of his chewed-up sandwich. "That kind of stuff only happens in books."

Weird, Anna thought. Why would Olivia lie about that? And what was she really doing here?

CHAPTER 28

ANNA

The next day was one of those days when anything that could go wrong did. And so Anna had made the logical choice: she was hiding in the girls' room.

"Anna, come out," Millie said from outside the stall. Anna pinched her lips together.

"I know you're in there," Millie said. "I can see your ratty shoes."

"Fine!" Anna threw open the door with a bang.

"It's not that bad, you know," Millie told her.

"Not that bad? Are you serious?" Anna said, squeezing her eyes shut. It was horrible. It was life-shattering. It was—all true.

No sooner had Anna's worn-out soles touched the linoleum of Winchester Academy that morning than she'd heard several pings of cell phones going off down the hallway. One by one, like falling dominoes. Except Anna's. Her phone had remained silent, for the first time in nearly forever. Heads had turned in her direction as she passed. She'd heard the muffled whispers. *Anna Craven's mom gives makeovers . . . to dead people!*

Now Anna walked over to the dilapidated bench against the bathroom wall and sat down, propping her chin in her hands.

"Who cares if they know your mom does makeup and hair for corpses?"

Anna looked at her in amazement. "Don't you get it? Until now, everyone loved my mom. Even the Ashbury twins went to her at the salon. But they won't anymore. This will hurt her business." *And people will think I'm a freak,* she silently added.

Of course, maybe she was a freak. After all, she texted dead people.

How much freakier could she be?

"Maybe we can make it into something cool," Millie suggested. "Like your mom is so great at her job that even the dead beg for her services."

"Nice try. Nobody will listen to us."

"Well, maybe they will if we send a text out and make it look like it's from Olivia."

"There's no way we can pull something like that off." Anna tore some toilet paper off a nearby roll and blew her nose.

"Sure we can. I'll take care of it. Just wait and see."

Anna managed a small smile. "Okay." Olivia had to be the one behind the texts: she was the only person who had seen Anna at the funeral home. She dabbed her face with a wet paper towel, tossing it in the trash on her way out.

The door closed with a bang.

And the door to the stall at the very far end of the bathroom opened.

. . .

After school Anna's phone pinged with the alert of a new mass text message.

Had Millie's plan worked? Biting her lip, she scrolled to the message.

OMG I touched a corpse, read the text.

Underneath was a picture of Anna. She gasped, dropping her phone.

Millie wouldn't do that to her. She was her friend. There had to be an explanation. Anna shook her head, trying to clear her mind, and bent down to pick up her phone on the sidewalk. The corner of the screen was cracked. *Great, just great,* she thought.

But the crack wasn't big enough to hide what was so blatantly staring back at her: herself. Poking a finger at a dead person. It was a photo from the day before.

Anna's heart hammered against her chest. She quickly closed the picture.

Out of nowhere, Olivia popped up, her face pinched and red. She shoved her pink-leather-cased phone in Anna's face. "Seriously?"

Anna looked at the screen. Millie's text had gone out.

Missing: Olivia Ashbury. Found at: Leavitt Funeral Home, looking for a new boyfriend

Anna would've laughed if she didn't already feel like crying.

"Me? You're the one who couldn't wait to text *everyone* about my mom!" Anna said, so upset she didn't even think to be scared to stand up to her.

Olivia glared at her. "Don't mess with me," she said. Then she spun on her boot heel and walked across the leaf-strewn schoolyard.

Anna sent a text to Millie.

Can you meet me at the graveyard in thirty minutes?

Yes!

When Anna got there, Millie was leaning against a tree. "So it sounds like Olivia isn't a fan of payback," Millie said.

"I guess we're even now," Anna said. "Except now everyone knows about my mom."

"It's really not that bad," Millie said. "And pretty soon something bigger will happen and it will take all the attention off you and nobody will remember a thing."

"I guess you're right," Anna said, sighing.

"So you really touched a dead person?" Millie asked.

Anna laughed. "I guess I just got caught up in the moment." Her phone buzzed with a new text.

"Hey, if that's from a ghost, I wanna read it!" Millie jumped up, peering over Anna's shoulder.

"Trust me, it's nothing to get excited over."

"It's a gift. You should embrace it," Millie said, her eyes wide.

"It's a curse, not a gift. Or else I would've given it back by now."

"Who's the text from?" Millie asked, trying to see the screen.

Anna read the message aloud. "*Need to talk to you. Now!* Who else? Lucy. My favorite ghost." She stuck the phone in her coat pocket.

"Aren't you going to see what she wants?"

"Whatever it is, it can wait," Anna said. She took a granola bar from her bag. "Want one?"

"No thanks," Millie said. "I'm not very hungry today."

A gust of wind blew through the graveyard, rustling the few leaves that remained on their branches.

Anna pulled her collar up, shivering. It was the weirdest thing.

She could've sworn she smelled lemons.

CHAPTER 29

ANNA

Millie was right: it wasn't long before people moved on. Occasionally someone would say "Dude! Touch any dead people today?" Anna barely batted an eye.

But there was no ignoring the paper taped to her locker that morning.

Her heart sank faster than the *Titanic*.

It was a photocopied page from her crazy great-uncle Maxwell Maddsen's journal.

One day this haunted old house will belong to my niece, Valerie Craven, and her daughter, Annabel.
I have a strange feeling

they'll be able to appreciate its ghostly past ... and future.

Anna couldn't have felt any worse if a boulder had crushed her flat as a pancake right there in the hallway.

Just then Johnny walked past. She hadn't seen him much lately. "Hey," he said.

"So now you know," Anna said, taking the paper off her locker.

"Know?" he repeated, wrinkling his forehead.

She waved the crinkled paper in his face. "Hello! Haven't you heard? I live in *the* Mad House. Maddsen is my *great-uncle*."

He rolled his eyes. "That's old news."

Anna looked at him in disbelief. "You knew?"

Johnny nodded. "You're not the only one with secrets around here."

"But why didn't you say something? Tell me that you knew?"

"I figured you'd tell me when you wanted to."

Anna's locker slammed shut behind her, making her whirl around. She caught a shimmer of the air and the familiar scent of lemons. It was Lucy.

"So this was your plan?" Lucy shouted at Anna. "To steal my boyfriend?" She stabbed the air with her index finger, punctuating each word.

"What?" Anna blurted out before clamping a hand over her mouth. She swiveled around to see Johnny staring at her.

"What's going on?" he asked her.

"Yeah, *Annabel,* why don't you tell him? Since I know you haven't really told him about me yet."

"Um . . ." Anna's eyes darted from Johnny to Lucy. And back to Johnny. If he hadn't thought she was a freak before, he certainly did now.

Lucy grabbed a handful of papers littered on the ground and threw the stack at Anna. Johnny's eyes widened as the papers magically seemed to hurl themselves through the air.

Gliding to Johnny's side, Lucy grabbed for his hand. Instead, her ghostly fingers passed right through his.

He shivered.

Lucy placed her mouth right next to Johnny's ear. "We can be together, John! Forever!" she cried.

"He's alive, not deaf," Anna said to Lucy, annoyed at her tantrum.

"What are you talking about?" Johnny looked as if he was getting angry. "Is this some sort of game you're playing?"

"What? No! It's Lucy—"

"Will you stop with the Lucy stuff?" He started to back away. "Because you know she's dead, right? And whatever you're trying to do, it's not funny."

"It's not me, Johnny. She's here right now. I didn't know how to tell you before without making it sound like I was crazy. . . ." Anna trailed off, realizing that was exactly how she sounded.

An echo of clanging metal sounded down the hallway as Lucy floated past each locker and, one by one, banged her fists against them.

"You're right about that," Johnny said, putting his palms face out. "I don't know how you're doing that, or why, but . . . maybe you are the freaky girl after all." With that, he turned and walked around the corner, out of sight.

Anna bit her bottom lip, her eyes welling up with tears.

"How's it feel now, boyfriend stealer?" Lucy reappeared in front of Anna with a Cheshire cat grin.

"Shut up, you stupid ghost!" Anna clenched her fists at her sides. "I swear I'll call the freakin' ghost hunters on your butt," she muttered under her breath.

Lucy's laughter echoed faintly down the hallway as she left.

CHAPTER 30

Lucy

Lucy eyeballed the Ashbury twins and their cookie-cutter look-alikes at the Corner Café. The best way to get to Johnny and Eden would be to infiltrate their group. And by infiltrate, she meant snatch one of their bodies. Temporarily, of course.

"Eeny, meeny, miney, moe, who will the lucky girl be?" Lucy chanted, pointing her finger at each girl in the booth and finally settling on Nessa Bloom. Über-rich, she pretty much had money coming out her pores. Or she would have, if she had pores . . . but she had a porcelain complexion that any girl would die for.

"Nessa it is!"

She silently glided to Nessa.

Olivia shivered. "It's freezing in here," she muttered. "Eden, go make sure the front door is shut."

"I can see it from here," she told her sister. "It is shut."

"It must not be closed all the way."

With a sigh, Eden dutifully walked over to the door.

"So what does the count look like for Fall Ball Queen, Nessa?" Olivia knew she was in the running, even though the dance wasn't until the end of the month. She just wanted to hear the confirmation.

Lucy wasn't exactly sure how this was done. *Here goes nothing.* She grabbed Nessa by the shoulders and tried to merge her ghostly glowing spirit into Nessa's body. Nessa jerked back and forth like she was having a spasm.

"Are you okay?" Eden looked concerned. She touched Nessa's arm. "Oh my God. You're so cold!"

"Of course she's okay. She thinks it's cute to ignore me," Olivia snapped.

"No, she really doesn't look well," a girl named Saffron said, clutching her purse, looking like she was ready to jet if Nessa threw up.

Lucy's body flung violently from Nessa's body, smacking right into Saffron. For whatever reason, Nessa's body was rejecting her. She tried merging into Saffron, but that didn't work either.

Olivia's blond brows furrowed. "Saff, do you know something about the voting that I don't? Because if you do and you're not telling me—"

"No. I just . . ." Saffron was shivering. "I just think you're right. It is really cold in here."

Eden scooted into the booth with them. "Nope. The door is definitely shut."

Lucy stared at Eden. Maybe she would be a little easier. Lucy floated straight into Eden, meshing with her body as one. Eden sputtered, shaking, coughing. Olivia rolled her eyes once more.

Taking Eden's body was as easy as a warm knife slicing through butter. Lucy smiled over at Olivia.

Olivia snorted. "What are you so happy about?"

And Eden, with Lucy inside her, laughed. "Life."

CHAPTER 31

ANNA

The stands were packed with students all fired up for the first big game of the season. Anna got a hot chocolate from the concession stand, then took a seat halfway up the bleachers. She hoped Millie and Spencer would decide to come.

Anna spotted Johnny's jersey number on the field. They hadn't spoken since Lucy went ghostal in the hallway. Whatever.

Just her luck: she saw Olivia down in front talking to the cheerleaders. Anna hoped Olivia didn't notice her among all the other people at the game.

The teams ran back and

forth, nobody scoring. Everyone in the stands was yelling, and for once Anna felt just like any other student, caught up in the school spirit.

Yo, Anna. Where are you?

It was Spencer.

Um, near a woman with a white pom-pom hat. 10th row up.

Anna felt like throwing her phone. The battery was almost drained. She had made sure it was fully charged before leaving for the game. Plus it was a new battery, so this shouldn't be happening still!

Seconds later Spencer was jogging up the steps toward her. "Hey," he said, grinning as he sat down next to her.

"Glad you made it," Anna said, smiling.

"Me too," Spencer said. "'Sup?"

"Not much." She took a sip of her hot chocolate. "How are the hauntings going?" she asked in a low voice.

"It's been kind of quiet lately."

"Lucky you." Things had been with Anna lately too, but she knew it wouldn't last. It was like the calm before the storm. The crowd around them cheered.

But then Anna saw something that made her heart stop.

"Oh no," she whispered.

Spencer looked over at her. "What's wrong?"

Without answering, Anna texted Millie.

> Guess who just showed up at the game? The creepy guy I saw in the cemetery on my first day!!!!! Don't meet me here, I'm leaving.

As she pressed the send button, her phone died. She hoped Millie got it in time.

"You feel like leaving?" Anna blurted out, already standing up. The creepy guy was standing with a blond girl, watching the game near the fence, his back to them. Was that Olivia?

"Already?" Spencer gave her a strange look. "Sure, why not."

They walked down the steps. Anna kept her head down. *Please don't see me, please don't see me,* she thought, nearly in a panic.

"Thanks for leaving with me," she said breathlessly as they walked past the concession stand.

"No big deal," Spencer said. "There'll be other games."

"Anna!" Millie waved as they reached the entrance.

She fell into step beside them. "Just got your text. Where are you going?"

Anna looked over at Spencer. "Corner Café okay with you?"

"Yep," Spencer said, watching other students as they passed.

"Can I go with you guys?" Millie asked.

"Sure," Anna said, glancing at Spencer, hoping he was okay with it, but he wasn't even paying attention. Obviously he couldn't mind too much.

"Cool!" Millie chirped.

Anna glanced over her shoulder as they walked through the parking lot. The creepy guy was nowhere to be seen.

But just in case, she quickened her step.

CHAPTER 32

Lucy

Lucy-as-Eden ran her hands down her perfectly fitting dress. Life couldn't get much better than this. She watched John play out on the football field. As the game ended, Lucy decided to make her move.

She gracefully walked down to the field in her high red heels.

"John," she whispered, bending down to his level.

He whipped his head around, then up, staring into her eyes. His eyes went wide as he saw how tall she suddenly was.

Obviously Eden doesn't wear these shoes often enough, Lucy thought.

"Oh. Hey, Eden." He appeared to be less enthusiastic than she'd expected. But she had to remember, he didn't know it was actually *her*.

Lucy bit back the urge to hug him. "I need to talk to you for a second."

"Uh, okay. I guess." Johnny looked behind him and nodded at his friends heading to the locker room. One of them swatted him on the butt. "Johnny, you're the *man*!"

He shivered as Lucy grabbed his arm and led him away from the crowds before stopping near the unoccupied bottom bleachers.

"Man, it's cold. So, uh, what's up?" he asked.

"It's *me*, John!" She could barely keep the excitement out of her voice.

He frowned at her. "Huh?" He tilted his chin over at a group of guys who were headed out. "Dude!"

"*No!*" she whispered, more impatiently this time. "It's me, *Lucy*."

He stared at her, then stepped back. "What did you say?"

"Look into my eyes," Lucy begged, moving toward him. "They're the windows to my soul."

He looked scared. He backed away farther.

"Johhhhn," she whined. "Remember when you gave me your phone number and picked me to be on your team for the class project? And—"

She placed a hand on his shoulder to help calm him, but it only made things worse.

"Don't touch me."

"Seriously, John. Don't make me keep haunting you every night. Now's your chance to talk to me. It can be like old times."

Awareness flickered over his face, as if he knew exactly what she was talking about. But it disappeared just as quickly. "I don't know what you're talking about." He broke into a jog toward his friends.

Furious, Lucy watched him go. "You don't want me to be your girlfriend anymore? Fine," she called after him.

If he wanted to pretend he didn't care, well . . .

She stomped her high heel on the concrete. "I wouldn't be your girlfriend ever again. You think you can hurt me? Over my dead body!" she yelled.

And she meant it.

CHAPTER 33

ANNA

Spencer and Anna walked into the Corner Café, the bell jingling as they opened the door. It was completely dead inside, with just two employees gossiping by the front counter.

As they sat down, Anna found herself thinking about the last time she had been here, with Johnny. She hoped they could be friends again. And then she thought back to the night of the Ashburys' party. Olivia had disappeared for a while, and Eden had been looking for her. Was it possible that Olivia had been gone long enough to get to the cemetery and back?

"I'm not really hungry, so go ahead and order something without me," Millie said as she stood up, heading back toward the restrooms.

Anna turned to Spencer. "I know this is really random, but I was thinking about something and wanted to see what you thought."

The server came to their table, and Anna ordered a Coke, her stomach too twisted in knots for food. Spencer did the same.

"What?" Spencer asked.

"Do you think it's possible that Olivia got Lucy to go to the cemetery that night?" Anna asked. "The night Lucy . . . died?"

"I don't know," Spencer said. "Why would she do that?"

"Maybe she was jealous?" Anna shrugged. "Or just wanted to play a mean prank."

Millie had returned. "I think that's possible," she said. "But who cares? It can't change what happened."

"Sorry," Anna said, twisting her napkin as the server brought over their drinks. "I just wanted to see what you thought. . . . I'll shut up now."

Millie laughed.

"Don't worry about it." Spencer took a sip of his soda.

The front entrance jingled, a cold blast of air flooding the room.

"Hey, Anna," Nessa said, smirking in her cheer uniform as she walked past their table. She ignored Spencer and Millie.

Anna's stomach dipped. She couldn't remember ever seeing Nessa without the clones around. She seriously hoped that didn't mean Olivia was on her way.

The café was slowly filling up with students. The game must have ended.

"Should we go?" Anna asked.

Spencer looked around. "Yeah, maybe . . ."

"Anna! You're here." Johnny was suddenly at their table, still in his football uniform. "I need to talk to you."

Anna sighed, scooting her chair back, the metal legs screeching along the tile. "Be right back." She followed Johnny to the back of the room.

"Lucy was at the game tonight," Johnny muttered under his breath.

"What?" Anna asked. "How?"

Johnny took a step closer to Anna. "Look, I believe you," he whispered. "Let's go back to your house. Together. I—I don't want to be alone in case she, uh, comes back."

Anna opened her mouth to say something but stopped herself. She needed to find Lucy and see what was going on.

She turned to Spencer and Millie. "Sorry, guys. I gotta go."

. . .

Johnny and Anna walked to her house in silence. She had borrowed Johnny's phone and sent several texts to Lucy.

> Hi, it's Anna. Please meet me at my house. I'm with Johnny. We want to talk to you.

The Manor was dark. Her mom was probably working at the funeral home again tonight. There were so many dead people around here.

Anna glanced over at Johnny as she unlocked the front door. She hoped he'd be able to deal with seeing Lucy.

Maybe tonight they'd all get the resolution they needed.

The house was silent. Anna was about to shut the door behind them when, to her surprise, Eden stuck her foot in the door. Shocked, Anna let go of the doorknob, and she walked right in.

"Eden? What are you doing here?" Anna asked, staring at the girl. She looked angry. Anna felt fear course through her veins. Something was definitely wrong here.

"So it's true," Eden said, walking toward Anna without shutting the door.

"What are you talking about?"

Eden glared at her. "Look, Anna. I know you're trying to turn John against me."

"Eden? What's wrong? This isn't like you," Anna said. Her eyes darted nervously to Johnny.

Johnny grabbed Eden's arm. "Hey—"

Eden flung Johnny's arm off hard enough to throw him off balance. He fell backward and crashed through the glass coffee table behind him, shattering it and landing unconscious on the floor.

Anna screamed.

Eden whirled on Anna. "I swear I didn't mean for that to happen! I didn't know I still had so much power even being stuck in this body!" she cried.

Anna gasped. "Lucy? Is that you?" She stared at her. "What did you do with Eden? You didn't . . ." Her voice trailed off.

"I didn't hurt Eden, I was just using her. And now look what I did." She let out a strangled half sob.

Anna looked down at Johnny, waiting for him to get up. But he didn't move.

Anna shook her head. "No, it was an accident. You . . . he . . ."

Tears were streaming down Eden's cheeks. "It's all my fault." She knelt down beside Johnny. "Wake up!"

"Is he—" Anna couldn't bring herself to ask the question. If Johnny was . . . gone, then she'd see his spirit. She was sure of it.

Eden suddenly jumped up. "He's breathing! He's okay! He's—"

Thump.

Anna steadied herself against the counter as there was a crack and Eden fell to the floor, unconscious. Millie was in the doorway, holding the remains of a now-broken vase.

"Millie!" Anna exclaimed, running to hug her friend. It had been brave of Millie to knock Eden out when she thought she was going to hurt Anna, but what about poor Eden? And was Lucy still inside?

Anna's shoes crunched on glass as she carefully picked her way across the floor. She could already see that Johnny was breathing, and his cuts didn't seem so bad from where she was, but she couldn't tell how much glass was beneath him. When she reached him she felt his pulse. It seemed strong, but he wasn't coming around. And she was afraid he might have hit his head when he fell. When he woke up, he was going to be in a lot of pain. She wasn't going to move him herself.

Anna pulled out her cell phone, then remembered

the battery had died. She checked it anyway—and now the screen was lit and glowing brightly. It showed full battery and perfect reception.

How is this happening? As Anna called for help, her eyes darted to Eden, who had started to groan, rolling over on her side and clutching her head. Lucy must still be inside her body, Anna realized. Her phone always worked perfectly around Lucy. Her eyes went wide as she remembered how her phone had done the same thing at the funeral home. And at the cemetery. It was as if energy from the spirits affected her phone. Or powered it. It always had the strongest reception around them. And away from them, the battery drained almost immediately.

And then a new scent tickled her nose. Anna knew Lucy smelled like lemons, not peppermint. And that scared her.

CHAPTER 34

ANNA

Anna scanned the ER waiting room, looking for a place to sit with Millie. A TV played quietly in one corner. Two seats close to it were empty, sandwiched between two sweating and shivering men. As one leaned forward and hacked out a cough, Anna understood why no one else had jumped at the prime location. She steered herself toward the other side of the room, the bland walls and the table of torn magazines suddenly much more appealing.

The scents of bleach and antiseptic mingled in the air, along with the cigarette smoke wafting off people returning from the smoking area. Cold air rushed in from outside as

217

the automatic doors continually slid open and shut. Anna hated hospitals as much as cemeteries. A heavy mouth breather wedged herself into a chair next to Anna. Anna leaned over to her right, in the opposite direction.

Since they'd arrived at the hospital, her nose had been flooded with way too many scents. Everything from lavender to mold. She hadn't smelled anything peppermint, and she hoped that was a good sign.

At the sound of a gurney being raised and a machine beeping, Anna glanced up.

That was when she noticed him. The guy from the cemetery.

"It's him! Creepy Vince," Anna croaked to Millie. She looked down at her feet, reminding herself she was in a public place.

He sat down in the chair on her right.

Anna's heart was racing. It was now or never. "Is there something you need?" she said, using her best I-dare-you-to-mess-with-me voice.

Vince shook his head, calmly picked up a teen magazine, and pretended to read. Like it was completely normal for stalkers to do this.

"What are you doing here, then?" Anna fired back. Who did he think he was fooling?

Vince slowly lowered the magazine, his lips drawn

in a straight line. He unfolded his legs, sat up, and carelessly tossed the magazine back onto the table. "It's really none of your business," he said. "But I'm here to see my brother."

Millie glanced at Anna, shaking her head.

Anna ignored her. "Right. And who's your brother?"

"As if you don't know."

Millie nudged Anna with her elbow. "Just forget him. He's not worth it."

"Why don't you tell me," Anna said.

"Johnny. Who else?"

Anna gasped. He was totally lying. He had to be. She looked over to Millie, but her face didn't register surprise. "You knew?" she whispered.

Millie shrugged, looking down at her feet. Suddenly her boot laces were the most interesting things in the room.

. . .

There was no way Anna was going to wait in the same room with that psycho. Even with Millie next to her, she was creeped out being so close to him. She could practically smell the evil coming off him in waves. She rushed out of the hospital, but Vincent followed her, with Millie close behind.

"It's my fault he's here," he said.

Anna couldn't possibly tell him the truth: that Lucy, a ghost, had caused the accident while inhabiting Eden's body. And even though she couldn't stand this slimy creep or even comprehend how he could possibly be related to Johnny in any way, she didn't think it was right that he felt responsible.

"Look, it's not your fault," Anna said.

Vincent stuffed his hands in his pockets, kicking his feet against the pavement. "If I hadn't agreed to help Olivia, then—"

"Help Olivia do what?" Anna blurted out.

"Get rid of Lucy."

Anna gasped. "What?"

Vincent furrowed his brows. "Not like that! She just wanted Lucy to lay off and quit bugging Johnny. She thought that if we could make her think Johnny had done something to embarrass her, then she would get lost."

"Nice," Millie said sarcastically.

"Olivia made Lucy *think* it was Johnny who was supposed to meet her that night at the cemetery. Olivia sent Lucy a text from Johnny's phone setting the whole thing up. She planned to scare Lucy to death when she showed."

"Well, it all went the way she planned, then," Anna said, barely keeping the disgust from her voice.

"Everyone knew Lucy had a huge fear of clowns. I gave Olivia an old Halloween mask and a flashlight. She hid in the cemetery. I'd left a shovel there earlier in the day . . . and that's where Lucy fell. She tripped over my shovel."

A clown mask. Like the picture on the phone I found. And I bet the flashlight was the bright light Lucy saw right before—

"That's not what made her fall," Anna said. "Olivia did scare her, but Lucy was wearing heels in the wet grass. And the ground was muddy. She even fell and twisted her ankle on her way to the cemetery that night."

"How do you know all that?"

Now she had blabbed too much.

Vincent shook his head. "Look, it doesn't matter. I just—well, Johnny just better come out of this okay." Vincent spun around and headed back toward the waiting room.

Anna turned to Millie. "The phone I found . . . I think it belonged to Vincent. And because Olivia made it a point to find out my name and classes before I started at school, I'm betting that's how he knew my name too. She must've told him."

"You think he was trying to get his phone back from you that first day?" Millie asked.

"That would make sense, right? He could've lost his

phone at work, so he just assumed the new girl walking through the cemetery was the one who found it. Or maybe Olivia put the idea in his head. Who knows?"

"But what's the big deal with the phone? Did he want it back so badly because the ghosts contacted him too?"

Anna laughed. "If that were true, he wouldn't want his phone back. I'm thinking it was because he had a picture of that mask on his phone."

"Oh, yeah. That could connect him to Olivia, who scared Lucy that night. And I bet those texts in the phone were from her too."

Anna sighed. "I think I'm going to go back in."

Millie nodded. "Yeah. I should be heading home, though. It's getting late."

"Okay. I'll text you later. Thanks for everything, Millie." She squeezed her hand. "You're a real friend."

Millie nodded. "You too, Anna."

• • •

Lucy-as-Eden arrived at Anna's house fifteen minutes after Anna texted her. Lucy didn't care about punctuality anymore. Besides, arriving late was always more fashionable. She already knew what Anna would say, and she was ready for it.

"Stop." Lucy held up a hand before Anna could get a word out. "I shouldn't have snatched a body. It's an invasion of privacy, people are entitled to their personal space, blah blah blah."

"So glad you learned your lesson," Anna said. She crossed her arms over her chest, waiting for Lucy-as-Eden to carry on.

"I am giving Eden her body back. I'm really not the sharing type. Besides, her nagging is giving me a killer headache."

"Nagging?" Anna echoed.

"Yeah. She keeps yelling at me to get out of her body, but I've learned to tune her out. It's like white noise now. Still . . . it's annoying." She shrugged. "I'd rather be free to float alone. It suits me."

"And promise no more haunting anyone?" Anna asked. Lucy knew who she was referring to.

"Yeah, yeah." She waved her hand dismissively. "I've seen enough to know he doesn't like me. But you know what? It's his loss. He's all yours."

Anna studied her. "The Lucy I know would never give up that easily. Don't tell me you met someone?"

Lucy sighed. "Calm yourself before you have an aneurysm and end up like me. But yes, I did. His name is Ricky. Well, I call him Rick." She smiled. "And don't worry, he's dead too."

"You didn't have anything to do with that, did you?" Anna asked, a worried look in her eyes.

Lucy shook Eden's head. "He's been a goner for a lot longer than I have. He even said he'll show me the ropes. I'm getting stronger, and I can stay visible for longer periods of time, but I definitely need help learning to control everything."

"Wow! That's great," Anna said. "So, um, when are you giving Eden her body back?"

"Now. Thanks for everything, Anna. It's been real." She gave a little wave right as her shoulders began to shake, her body convulsing.

"Wait! Lucy!" Anna cried. But it was too late.

. . .

Eden blinked several times at Anna, looking dazed. "Where am I?" she whispered.

"Wow," Anna said, throwing her arms wide. She couldn't believe Lucy had left her to explain everything.

Eden looked down at her body, waving her hands in front of her face, her eyes glazed over.

"Eden?"

She turned her head slowly toward Anna, a blank stare on her face.

"You okay, Eden?" What if Eden blamed her for everything? What if she had some sort of permanent damage from Lucy's taking over like that? Anna was at a complete loss as to what to do.

Eden shook her head slowly, as if it took every ounce of effort to move it. "What . . . why do I feel so weird?"

Anna tilted her head to the side. "You don't remember?"

"Remember what?" She sat down on the edge of Anna's bed.

"Uh . . . that you've been sick."

"Sick?"

"Yeah. You said you were feeling dizzy and needed to lie down."

"Oh. Have I been here long?"

"Not that long. We were just studying." Anna hoped she wouldn't notice the lack of books and backpacks.

"So we're at your house?" Eden started to loosen up a little and move more easily as her eyes skimmed over the few items in Anna's small room.

Anna sighed. "Yeah."

"Well, I probably already said this and don't remember, but your room is amazing! Love the color."

"Yeah? I always figured you for a pink kind of girl." Anna wanted to see how she would respond.

Eden giggled. "Pink is definitely more Olivia than me. Hey, it looks like your clock isn't working." She pointed to the black wall clock above Anna's bed. She still hadn't taken it down since moving in.

"It's probably been like that for a while. All the old clocks in this house are stuck at twelve o'clock."

"Midnight?" Eden's eyes widened, turning to Anna. "That's the witching hour."

"What does that mean?"

"It's the time of day when powerful beings are at their strongest."

"Oh." Anna didn't know how else to respond.

"It's okay. Not a lot of people know. I'll show you what I mean sometime." Eden beamed.

"Um . . . sure?" Anna tried to keep her voice steady as her whole body tensed up.

No way! Anna screamed in her head. *I draw the line at ghosts!*

CHAPTER 35

ANNA

So maybe the graveyard wasn't *the* absolute worst place ever.

Anna held a bouquet of sunflowers tightly in her hands and Millie carried daisies as they walked slowly through the wet grass between the headstones. The sun was covered by swirling gray clouds. Anna pulled her coat tighter around her body, hoping to get out of there before the weather got worse.

Anna had texted Millie to meet her here. She didn't think she could do this alone.

They paused to visit their favorite nagging spirit.

Lucy Edwards.

Millie placed the daisies on top of Lucy's name on the headstone. Lucy probably would never even see these, but if she did, Anna was sure she'd complain that they should've brought more. Or they weren't expensive enough.

"Do you think she'll ever bother you again?" Millie asked.

"Probably," Anna said. "Someone like Lucy doesn't go away that easily. Besides, I think there are still things tying her here. And you know how stubborn she is. I'm sure she'll think of a reason to come back."

They were strolling down the path through the graveyard when Millie suddenly stopped.

"Okay, I have to confess. I hope you won't be mad at me, but . . ."

"Spill it." Anna waited for her friend to gather her courage.

"Well, you know that rose you found in your locker that one day?"

"Uh-huh."

Millie raised her hand. "Guilty."

"That was you? Why?"

"I knew how horrible Olivia could be, and I figured that if you thought she was behind it, then you'd stay away from her."

"But—but that only freaked me out like the other things!"

"I know. I'm sorry! Wait, what other things?"

Annabel took a deep breath. "You know, the pic of Lucy torn from the yearbook."

Millie shook her head. "That wasn't me. But I'm pretty sure it was Olivia. She's been known to do stupid stuff to intimidate people."

They continued walking through the grass. "Next time just talk to me. Dead roses with blood are just creepy, 'kay?"

Millie nodded, glancing down at the flowers Anna still held. "So what are you doing with those?" Her voice sounded shaky.

"Remember when you were out sick that day and I tried texting you but you had lost your phone?" Anna asked.

"And you got it back for me," Millie remembered.

"Yeah." Anna nodded. "I also tried to find your house that day to bring it to you."

"Really?" Millie looked down at her feet. "I didn't know that."

"I remembered you mentioned the street you lived on, so I went there and . . . there were no houses."

"Oh, I must've told you the wrong street." Millie let out a forced little laugh. "You know me, always getting things mixed up!"

"You didn't mix anything up." Anna stopped walking and looked at Millie sadly. "It's just that your house had been in a fire. It burned to the ground. There was only one survivor. Your parents weren't home when it happened, but you and your older brother were. Your brother escaped. . . ."

"No, that's not right." She looked worried and confused. "We both got out of there and—"

Anna cut her off. "Millie, you've been my best friend since I moved here. But I've been so worried about my life and my drama and just trying to fit in that I—"

"You've been my best friend too," Millie insisted.

"But I was stupid. I didn't really pay attention. Or didn't want to." Tears blurred Anna's vision, but she didn't wipe them away when they coursed down her cheeks. "I guess I was just so focused on me that when I finally did figure it out, I didn't want it to be true."

"You weren't stupid, Anna. It's hard to fit in at a new place."

"Millie. It's okay. *I know.*"

"I don't know what you mean."

"Yes, you do." Anna took a deep breath and gently laid the sunflowers beside the headstone at her feet, which read:

MILLICENT MARGUERITE MADDSEN
1933–1947

Millie shook her head wildly. "No."

Anna swallowed the lump in her throat and turned to face her friend. She put a hand on Millie's arm and fought the icy sensation that crept through her fingers.

"You're dead, Millie. I found the article in the library about that fire. Maxwell tried to save you, but . . ." Anna's voice cracked. "He wrote about it in that journal I found too. When they moved to the Manor, you did too. He was able to see you and talk to you. Just like me . . ."

"I don't want to hear this," Millie mumbled.

"It's like what Lucy went through."

"I'm not delusional. . . ."

Anna laughed. "No, but you're in denial. You don't want to accept your fate . . . but you have to, Millie."

Anna let go of Millie's arm and watched as her spirit knelt on the ground beside her own grave and traced the outline of the engraved words with the tip of her finger. Slowly her shape began to fade. She sighed, looking anxiously up at Anna. "I'm not ready to move on," she whispered.

"I'm not ready to say goodbye." Anna reached out toward Millie, blinking back tears.

Millie's once-solid form shimmered around the edges for several seconds before completely vanishing. The sweet smell of vanilla lingered.

Anna covered her face with her hands. Millie wasn't just her best friend, she was family. Her great-aunt! There were so many things she wanted to know. And they still had yet to go into town and see a movie, and go shopping, and do all those things best friends are supposed to do.

Best friends who are human, she reasoned with herself.

With a deep breath, she dug her hands into the soft ground and made a small hole. She pulled the brightly glowing phone from her pocket and tossed it in, then covered it back up. She patted her hand firmly over the fresh mound and wiped her hands on her jeans.

Then she walked up the path that led to her house, never looking back at the graveyard, and never noticing the dark figures that loomed there.

Ghosts really do exist, she thought. *And I communicate with them.*

She knew Millie would find a way to contact her again. Anna just hoped the same couldn't be said about other ghosts.

Too bad nothing stays buried forever.

ACKNOWLEDGMENTS

I have wanted to write this story forever (about ten years). Through all the many, many changes, wonderful people have supported me, and there are a few who deserve a special thanks. Because without you, it would still just be an idea haunting me.

My husband, Carl, and my boys, Christian, Alexander, and Sammy. You understood that when I kicked you out of my room to write, I did it with love. And when I jumped out of dark corners to scare you, it was solely for the purpose of research.

Ann Marie Meyers and Mindy Alyse Weiss, you helped back when this story was just a confession from a mortician's daughter. You both were incredibly supportive through my tears and my celebrations. And my tears. But we won't mention that.

My brother, Brandon, for sharing the real-life experiences with me and never laughing at me (to my face) when I tried to hunt for ghosts. I promise not to haunt you in the afterlife. Maybe.

Amie Borst and Niki Moss, two incredible writers and fantastic friends. You helped me in so many ways when I hit a block or needed an extra push of creativity. And you never once complained. What's your secret?

Kari Ripplinger, my bestie (living), who came to my rescue when I sprained my finger during a deadline. I love you like I love chocolate. And that's a lot!

Rosemary Stimola, my wonderful agent, it is because of you that I'm able to share my stories with the world. What would I do without you? Please don't answer that.

Wendy Loggia and the whole amazing team at Random House, thank you for all the hard work and dedication that made this story into an actual book.

ABOUT THE AUTHOR

Rose Cooper is the author/illustrator of *Gossip from the Girls' Room, Rumors from the Boys' Room,* and *Secrets from the Sleeping Bag.*

When Rose was a teenager, she moved to a tiny town, where her stepdad was a mortician, her mom was a corpse cosmetician, and their house was on cemetery grounds. She lives in Sacramento, California, with her family and makes sure all her texts are to the living.

Visit her at Rose-Cooper.com.

Follow Rose Cooper on